**WARNING:** In *Ariel's Super Power of Love: The Erotic Wonders of a Super Heroic Woman,* Ariel pushes her own boundaries redefining what's right and wrong in every situation, including the bedroom. Her journey of lace and lingerie includes solo F, M/F, F/F, M/F/M/M, and a stage performance that would make Miley Cyrus blush. For 18 years and older.

·

# WHAT READERS ARE SAYING...

"A wild and crazy run! Ariel's adventures kept me turning pages long into the night just to find out the next outrageously fun and sexy thing she'd do. She had her dark moments, too, but make no mistake, Ariel's story is a romance with an unusual happily ever after."

**~Jasmine Haynes, Author of *The Jackson Brothers* series and *Open Invitation* series**

"I started reading at 11 PM, figuring I'd read for a half hour and then go to sleep. Finally, at 3 AM, I forced myself to put my Kindle down. (A girl has to sleep, after all!) Yes, it's that good."

**~Karysa Faire, author of *Swashbuckler* and *Siren's Opus***

"The scenes are steamy and they will make you blush. I highly recommend taking the book to bed with you."

**~Ana Galvan, author of *The Contents of Desire***

# ARIEL'S

# SUPER POWER

# OF LOVE

## THE EROTIC WONDERS
## OF A SUPER HEROIC WOMAN

A Short Novel

Liz Adams

ARIEL'S SUPER POWER OF LOVE
THE EROTIC WONDERS OF A SUPER HEROIC WOMAN

Published by: Barany Publishing
ISBN-13: 978-1-944841-00-3

# CHAPTER 1

A LOUD clanging sound jarred me awake. The sound came from a flight attendant pushing a beverage cart through the aisle. I woke up from my nap only to realize I'd rested my head on the shoulder of the handsome blond-haired, blue-eyed passenger sitting next to me.

"Oh! *Izvinitye,*" I apologized in Russian over the din of the plane's engines.

He replied in Russian with a cute smile, full of sparkling teeth. "No, no. It's okay. You can rest your head on my shoulder if you're tired. You speak Russian?" Based on his accent, I placed him as someone born South of St. Petersburg, our destination.

"I studied it in school." At least I was partly honest. I threaded a loose lock of my raven black hair

1

behind my ear. I couldn't exactly tell him that I learned two dialects of Russian, along with martial arts, firearms, and high tech in a secret government facility from age fifteen onward. "Where are you from?" I continued in Russian. My voice fought against the hum of the plane and the passengers talking behind us.

"Veliky Novgorod, a city South of St. Petersburg." He scratched the cute five o'clock shadow. He had been clean-shaven at the beginning of our twelve-hour transatlantic flight with a four-hour layover in Paris. He looked fit and trim, and all over yummy.

"Why were you in the US?" I asked.

"My uncle got married. I went to his wedding."

"Oh, that's lovely." I admired his sapphire eyes. He had the kind of eyes that seemed to say, *I'm here for you.*

"Are you American?" He asked.

"Yes. Born and raised in Kansas."

"And your parents? Were they also born in America?"

A fist of hurt bit into my heart. The insignia of two arrows and a sickle branded on my father's forehead flashed in mind.

Kind Eyes took my hand. "What's wrong?"

"Nothing, it's just…." I let him hang on to my hand. "My father had an accident and died when I was a teenager."

2

"I'm so sorry."

"It's okay." I smiled sadly. "When I was a kid, I used to hate going to church. On those Sunday mornings when I rebelled against going, Dad would say, 'But Ariel, you'll get to do communion and drink wine. With enough wine, you can get drunk and look like this.' Then he'd put this drunken smile on his face and stumble all over the room until I was rolling on the floor laughing."

"Sounds like a wonderful father. A good man."

I nodded. God, I missed Dad so much. "After he passed away, I never could bring myself to taste wine again. Any alcoholic drink, really." I shrugged and stared past his shoulder out the window into the dark.

He stroked my hand in soothing circles. "That's okay. Alcohol is overrated anyway. Don't let anyone in my country know I said that, though." He smiled and I let in the love he offered me in his warm gaze. "Your mother is still alive?"

"Yes. Alive and well."

"Where is she from?"

I didn't think telling him that my mother was a different species would go over well.

"Canada," I lied. Needing my space to think of my mother, I took my hand away from him and touched my necklace.

"Oh. I'm sorry." He scowled.

Damn. When I took my hand away, he probably

3

thought I wasn't interested in him. I needed to offer back my hand.

A flight attended appeared. "*Napitok?* Beverage?"

"*Nyet*," I said hoping to rid of her as quickly as possible. "*Spasibo.*"

Once the flight attended moved on to the passengers sitting behind us, I turned to my neighbor hoping to connect with him again, but I was too late. He had shifted in his seat and leaned his head against the window to sleep.

I sighed and rubbed the triangular medallion on my silver chain – a gift from my mother, and the symbol of her tribe hidden away in the African jungle.

The deep rumble of the jet engines hummed as the plane soared over the Baltic Sea. The smell of cold recycled air wafted.

Nearly one hundred years ago, the US stumbled upon my tribal ancestors, the men and women who sported increased muscle density from a millennia of evolution. When the American explorers realized they had stumbled upon a new species of Hominid, they became thrilled at the chance of making the discovery of the century. Wishing to remain an unknown culture, our tribal leader asked the US explorers what it would take to not expose the tribe's existence to the rest of the world. The government requested to have one of the members of the tribe to study. The tribe offered an expendable member of their species. A woman named Wendistra. My mother.

After studying her feats of strength and her physiology, the US included her on military missions. Though the government had every intention of keeping my tribal ancestors a secret, word leaked out somehow. Fortunately, the truth got skewed and found its way into comic books as Wonder Woman and other cultural media. My mother is nothing like the Wonder Woman character portrayed in the comics. She has no costume, no bracelets, no magical rope. The only thing the fictional superhero has in common with my mother, Wendy, is that they're both strong.

My mother married a human, Cyril Garrison, my Dad. Though I'm a hybrid, I've inherited the genetic high muscle density trait. I may look like a thin girl, but I weigh a lot more than I look. Ever since I was fifteen-years-old, I've been trained for missions of war. In the near future, once I finish college, I'll be taking my mother's place, starting with national assignments before moving on to international missions.

The cute guy next to me was asleep. I wished he were awake. He had such sexy blue eyes. Whoa! What was that stirring at his pants? I've been forever impressed by how men can get hard-ons while they're asleep. His was still growing.

My nipples were doing their own growing. Glad no one was seated on the other side of me, I spread a blanket over my body and spooned in his direction. I hoped that all the movement I caused with getting the blanket over me would wake him up, but it didn't.

Didn't matter. I didn't need to wait for him. Underneath the blanket, I released the clasp at the back of my bra. That freed my breasts. I sighed. I cradled my breasts, skin on skin. With a gentle glide of my fingertips, my nipples perked up making me wet and yearning for more. I unsnapped the top of my jeans and zipped it open. I snuggled a finger between my folds. Putting the finger to my mouth, I tasted my tart self. I tucked my glistening finger back underneath and found my clit. I soothed her and stroked her in long, loving circles, imagining it was this man's finger soothing me, stroking me. The more I touched, the more swollen she became, demanding more.

My body started feeling it was on its own flight. I rose higher and muffled a moan.

The yearning to be scratched sunk inside me. I pushed my finger past my entrance to find it. My body lifted higher at my touch. I squeezed my breast with my other hand. The yearning to be scratched dove further, so I pushed my finger deeper.

A glance at the huge rod in my neighbor's pants was all I needed to imagine him inside me, pumping me. I inserted another finger. I was practically writhing on my hand, but satisfying the yearning eluded me still, wanting more.

This was ridiculous. I wouldn't be content until I

had him inside me.

I spread the blanket over the both of us. With a gentle touch, I ran my fingertips along his length.

He lifted his tired eyes. His shocked, pleased expression that followed was priceless.

I gave him a squeeze. "We'll arrive in about an hour. Are you up for getting to know each other better?"

He didn't say anything. He just opened his fly and gave me direct access. I gripped his hot flesh. He made a quiet groan of gratitude.

Hey! This wasn't just about him.

I guided his hand to my open jeans and he got the hint.

We sat like that for a good fifteen minutes, staring into each other's eyes, letting our fingers do the talking. Though my body was flying to new heights, and my panties were soaked with desire, I needed more.

"Let's take this to the bathroom. Meet me there in two minutes." I kissed his cheek, zipped up my pants, and straightened my hair.

My Conscience, poor girl, was probably trying to shout how joining the mile-high club was not a good idea. I couldn't hear her, though. My body's dominating desire for sex had tied her to a chair and held a knife to her throat.

I stood on wobbly legs to open the overhead compartment and retrieved the little packet I needed from my carry-on. I braced myself on the top of passengers' seats, supporting myself on the move to the back of the plane.

# CHAPTER 2

A T LAST, I got to feel those lips of his against mine. Though it was cramped in the tiny bright restroom, I welcomed the challenge. The craving itch in my core continued its screaming, but I was just seconds away from having his throbbing scratcher inside me.

His tongue darted across my lips and into my mouth. I sighed into him. He tasted as sweet as he looked. What would it be like to come home to a beautiful man such as this man, greeting me each day by holding me as tight as this embrace, kissing me as passionately as these lips?

This man. This embrace. These lips.

He broke the kiss, panting a little. My own breath heaved as much as his.

What would it be like to have him in my life where I could call him whenever I had a rough day or just needed someone to talk to? To wake up each morning in the comfort of his strong arms?

He smiled. "I'm Dimitri."

"Nice to meet you, Dimitri. I'm Ariel."

"A pleasure to meet you, Ariel." He pressed his lips against mine once again, and squeezed my breast to a happier place.

My nipple squealed with delight. Or perhaps that was me. I ran my hands up his shirt and lost myself in the forest of his chest hair and hot skin. We staggered in our standing embrace, adjusting to the cramped quarters. He held me closer. I relished the feel of his chest against my palm.

I broke the kiss to catch my breath, our lips still practically touching.

"You're gorgeous," I breathed.

I felt him smile against my lips.

*Dimitri.* I would come home each day to Dimitri. He would care for me, admire me, adore me, and love me. And be inside me, the way I needed him to be inside me now.

I reached into his jeans and wrapped my fist around his length. The more I squeezed him, the more he filled with his need for me, becoming harder in my hand. He groaned, then stepped back, yanking my jeans down to my ankles. As he crouched at my feet, I stepped out of my pants, forcing off my tennis shoes, my heart running laps at the thought of what was next.

What would it be like to go out to a rock concert together? To hold hands as the music took us on a spiritual journey? Then come home ripping each other's clothes off to celebrate the music's passion in other ways?

He stood and granted me another taste of his lips, his tongue, his desire. He propped my leg on the lid of the seat. My lips opened to the cool air, but he moved quickly to cup my mound, a finger sliding between my folds. With his other hand he raised my blouse and planted his mouth against my breast.

I moaned and gyrated slow circles on his hand, swiveling my hips as his fingertip swirled around my budding clit. That wasn't the spot that itched the most, but who was I to complain?

He covered good ground on my breast, streaking the full nipple and areola with his agile tongue, and had the good sense to follow the unspoken golden rule: whatever is done to one breast, do unto the other as well.

What would it be like to have this talented lover at my breast daily? Savoring me, tasting me, exploring me as though each day my body was new to him?

I embraced his head to my chest and fought with my knees to stay up as he melted away the rest of me with that single fingertip between my legs. I found the strength inside to push away his head and look into those lovely, kind eyes. "I want you inside me."

That got him moving fast. He freed his cock from his pants and directed it to my core. As much as I cherished the idea of having him and his children, I could never have unprotected sex.

I stopped him in time, sat him down, and plucked a foil packet from my jeans pocket, the one from my carry-on. He flashed a brief scowl, but thankfully didn't ask what kind of woman takes condoms with her on a plane. I covered him with the protection.

Squatting over him, I balanced myself above, rekindling our embrace. I lowered myself over his tip slowly. He had raised me to such heights, my desire dripped for him. He slipped into my entrance.

Here I was with a beautiful man. It would be so easy to devote all of me to him.

I slid further down, just enough to feel a bit more of him inside me and more of my sizzling need for him. We captured each other's eyes. My soul sank.

I didn't want any other eyes in my life.

I slid down further, letting him completely penetrate my core and puncture my heart. He filled me.

What would it be like to spend each night sharing one bedroom? To have him undress me and kiss me? To hold me in our bed? Our bed. I wanted that so much. To be able to say "our bed."

My throat choked at the longing of saying those two little words. I held him close to me and rested my head on his shoulder. He stirred himself inside me. My body gave in to the heat that began to simmer.

I ground against him. He held me tighter, moving with me. I didn't want this moment to end. He tucked his hand between us and caressed my breast. My nipple tightened to his touch, triggering new life across my sensitive skin. He swiveled his hips in faster circles. I cried out. My muscles contracted.

I twisted and writhed on him, feeling him embrace me tighter as I moaned my release and shook in his arms. He growled and pounded into me, coming to meet me. I spun down from my climax as he pushed his final thrusts deep inside.

Then we collapsed into our embrace. And as the world around us reappeared, as his length softened in me, we sat still clutching onto each other for one minute.

Two minutes.

Three.

Then time didn't matter. It was just us.

No one else mattered.

He kissed me with those spicy, loving lips of his. When our lips separated, our eyes locked. He stroked my hair. I shivered in the afterglow of our lovemaking.

He placed a gentle hand on my cheek. "Where are you staying? We must do this again."

I bit my lip. There was no easy way to say it. It—we—could never be. My throat tightened but I managed to get the words out in a soft even tone.

"I'm sorry. I just can't."

He jerked his head back as if he'd been slapped.

"I had a lovely time, though." And I meant it. I kissed his cheek and inhaled his male rich scent one last time. I straightened my clothes, not looking at him, and turned to the door. "Let's get back to our seats. We should be landing soon."

AS THE PLANE made its way above the Russian landscape, Dmitri didn't say much. I guess I broke his heart.

I decided to at least try to end our acquaintance on friendly terms.

Looking past him out the window, I pointed to the green square below us. "Check out the pretty park down there. Do you know what it is?"

"It's Lesopark Aleksandrino."

I feigned interest while he told me everything he knew about the park. He needed a distraction. I could tell. He wore a shell-shocked face, probably still dealing with the cold way I dismissed his request of staying in touch. Poor guy.

After we landed and rolled down the long runway at Pulkovo International Airport, the flight attendant welcomed us to St. Petersburg and announced it was "okay to take off our seatbelts," "be cautious when opening the overhead bins as luggage may have shifted," and all the other words flight attendants say when reciting the arrival chant. Everyone stood up at once. I opened the above bin and removed my luggage. The aisle was crowded so I didn't have a place to set the luggage down. I had to keep the bag over my head.

Dmitri saw my dilemma. "Here, let me help you with that."

Should I let him help? He might think I was giving him the cold shoulder if I declined. I handed him the bag. "Thank you."

He dropped the bag, probably hundreds of pounds too heavy for him, right on his toes. His poor toes.

I touched his arm. "Are you alright?"

He squeezed out tense words, perhaps to hide his pain. "I'm fine."

# CHAPTER 3

I DISEMBARKED with the other passengers. They all smelled like chain smokers, their clothes reeking of cigarettes. I met with the chaos of passport control. Though ten booths were available for passport control, only five were open: three for Russian citizens and VIPs, the remaining two for the rest of us. Without any extendable tape to help people form clear lines, people crowded around the passport control booths waiting for the booth's green light. Then passengers pushed to be next in line.

For all the talk of how beautiful St. Petersburg was, the airport looked run down. I had heard the city had plans to build a new international terminal, and now I could see why. The terminal was crowded, noisy, and bleak. As I waited among the masses for the passport control in the warehouse-sized room, I filled out the immigration form. Excitement was defined as moving forward three feet instead of one.

All of a sudden, a woman screeched in Russian. "My purse! Someone stole my purse!"

I quickly scanned the room. The surrounding passengers craned their necks to see who shouted.

All but one.

In the distance, a man clutching a purse at his waist hustled at a fast walk toward the exit. He was the only person who ignored the woman.

I bent down and discreetly ripped off one of the hockey-puck-sized wheels from my baggage. A girl who looked to be four years old watched me with big eyes. No one else seemed to notice what I was doing. I stood upright and flung the wheel across the room. With enough speed, even a wheel as small as this one could spin like a Frisbee. It arced over everyone and landed with a muffled crack at the back of the thief's head. He went down.

As the crowd sorted out that this fallen man had the screaming woman's purse, I put on a startled expression, pretending to be just as astonished as everyone else.

The little girl opened her mouth in a silent "O," staring at me with wonder. Was she impressed by my strength at removing and throwing the luggage wheel? Was that a glimmer of admiration in her eyes?

*Don't wish to be like me*, I imagined saying to her.

*My life is not as wonderful as you might think.*

I remembered the first time I felt the pain of who I was. At fourteen years old, as my mother and I walked away from the burial ceremony of my dad, she declared bitterly his death was her fault. I knew she was right and for several months I stopped talking to her. Even when I did speak to her again, I stopped calling her "Mom." I respected her, but I no longer felt like we were family. Calling her "Mother" was the best she could ever hope from me.

I was there when Dad died. Mother was not. I was there when members of a Russian mafia zoomed up in their black SUVs, and dumped my dad's broken, dying body onto the sidewalk in front of our house. I was there when they drove away with squealing tires as I rushed to his side. I was there when he smiled at me, revealing his broken teeth and a symbol burned into his forehead, like a brand. It was a symbol of a scythe cutting two arrows.

I was there when he whispered through his pain, "Remember that I love you. I always will. And tell your mom I love her, too."

I was there when he tried to soothe me with gentle shushing not to cry, that it was okay, that everything would be okay.

It was not okay. It would never be okay again.

I knew the source of the pain. He loved me. He loved Mother. The men who tortured him were not even trying to get any information out of him. They only did so to taunt my mother, to get back at her for destroying a drug trafficking hub, their main source of revenue in Florida.

Mother had said Dad's death was her fault? She was right. If Mother hadn't loved him, he wouldn't have been in danger. He would still be alive. Though I quickly realized that without their love I wouldn't have been born, the message was still loud and clear.

If I loved anyone, I would put them in jeopardy. I took after my mother, with the super strength and all. My life had to be a life of solitude. I could have sex with anyone I wanted to, I could just never have a relationship. I could never love a man, not without putting him in mortal danger. I could never have a life with a sweet, handsome man like the one on the plane.

I eyed the young girl waiting in line with me, and then turned away from her to watch the slow-moving line. To be like me would mean never letting anyone into your life. I wouldn't wish that on anyone.

I carried my hobbled suitcase the rest of the way.

# CHAPTER 4

THIRTY minutes later, after letting several people cut ahead of me, I was finally at the front of the line. When the green light came on to signify that the next person could enter the passport control booth, I pushed ahead and went in.

The agent, a burly man with just a shrug of mahogany hair, spoke English with a thick accent. "Passport and immigration card please."

I handed him my papers.

He compared my passport photo to my face with quick glances, flipped through the pages, then stared at my passport. "Name?"

"Ariel Garrison."

"Date of birth?"

"Six – eleven – ninety-one."

"Purpose of visit?"

"I'm an exchange student with Vassar University."

"How long do you plan to stay?"

"I plan on staying for six months."

"Where will you be staying?"

"A private residence in St. Petersburg."

"Relatives? Friends?"

"Uh, neither. The European University found the place for me to stay."

"Welcome to St Petersburg."

By the way he didn't look at me, I knew he didn't mean it.

With a hammy fist, he stamped the departure section of the immigration card. Kachunk! He tore off and kept the arrival section of the card, and returned the departure section to me along with my passport. I knew that when I planned to leave the country, if I wanted to get out without hassle, I needed to hang on to that stamped departure card to show how long I had stayed. Having passed his interrogation, the agent pressed a button, the door beside me clicked, and I left the booth.

Ten minutes later, I grabbed my luggage at baggage claim and snailed through customs. Another thirty minutes later—not so bad—I pushed my luggage cart through the crowd out to the eager people in the airport hallway, waiting for their spouse, friend, lover, or cousin. I scanned the crowd, finally spotting a tall man holding a sign with my name on it. Next to him stood a woman shorter than him.

As I approached them, the man said, "Ariel Garrison?"

"Yes."

What a relief it was to be met at the airport. I felt taken care of by the University, like I was in good hands. Both of them also smelled like heavy smokers. I realized the scent was a pattern I'd have to get used to. At least the cold air would chill and diminish the odor. Thank goodness I had the sense to request a host family that didn't smoke.

They introduced themselves in accented English as Svetlana and Leonid, representatives of the University's student exchange program.

Leonid shook my hand with a broad, friendly smile. Svetlana shook my hand with a cold, limp touch, and no smile. More like a grimace. I peered into her icy blue eyes and suppressed a shiver.

In her pleated navy blue skirt and white blouse, Svetlana looked me up and down disapprovingly. I'd seen that look before, especially in my last years in high school. It was a look that said, "You probably only succeeded because you slept with someone."

Her attitude infuriated me. I had worked hard to get into this program. I had worked my damn ass off—long study nights, weekends spent studying instead of partying with my classmates. Maybe she thought I got into the program because of my chocolate eyes and ruby lips, and not because of my grades. Maybe she even thought I had sex with the dean to get placed. If that was what she thought, she could go diddle herself. I turned my back on her to ignore her.

Leonid took my cart and told me they were going to drop me off at the apartment building of the host family. As we walked to the car I admired his lavender button-up shirt above a pair of solid blue jeans. He made small talk with me, and his waves of rich brown hair bounced as we made our way through the enormous open parking lot. When he opened the trunk, I quickly hefted my two large bags into it before he had a chance to offer to do it himself. I sat in the back of the tiny car enjoying the rare opportunity of being chauffeured. Still, the idea that Svetlana in the front passenger seat probably thought I used my body to get ahead angered me.

I huffed out the angry fire inside and tried to dismiss it. "I want to thank you for all your help."

"No problem." Leonid spoke cheerfully.

I felt the need to prove my competence. "I just want you to know that I'll work very hard to get good grades."

Svetlana sneered. "Of course you will."

What was that supposed to mean? As if reading my mind, Leonid replied keeping his eyes on the road. "What she means is we'd be surprised if you didn't get good grades."

Was that supposed to be a compliment? Or did they both think I took advantage of my professors by offering my body? I would never do that.

I kept silent for the rest of the trip.

# CHAPTER 5

E VER since I had learned that my dad's killer had his base of operations at some restaurant in St. Petersburg, I had wanted to come here to exact my revenge. My mother forbade it. She said revenge was wrong and immoral. At the time, I didn't care. But years passed and my anger dwindled.

Now that I sat here in the back seat of this car driving through the streets of St. Petersburg, I had no desire to seek out revenge. My heart resided in a place of peace. When I had first signed up for the foreign exchange program, I originally tried applying for Paris. I had a lot of competition. Getting to be a foreign exchange student in Paris was a long shot. When my educational counselor saw I had listed Russian as one of my fluent languages, she suggested I apply for

Russia's most beautiful city, St. Petersburg. I wasn't about to tell her that my dad got executed by a Russian mafia who kept their headquarters in St. Petersburg, but since revenge had dropped from my agenda, I followed my counselor's advice. I could now enjoy all the beauty the city had to offer.

Tall apartment buildings lined the city streets. The towering apartments ranged from grimy to colorful and reminded me of New York City. Five-and-dime stores occupied the sidewalk levels of the buildings and displayed Andy Warhol-like pop art signs with Russian words advertising their household goods, fruits and vegetables, sodas and snacks, all at special prices. Capitalism was alive and thriving.

Leonid and Svetlana drove me to a tower near a hotel called Hotel Solo on Furshtatskaya Street. The hotel name merely reminded me of how much I already missed my friends back home. After we stepped out of the car, Leonid opened the trunk and hoisted my first piece of luggage onto the sidewalk, making a poor attempt at hiding the strain of it.

"I'll take my carry-on," I said. Before he could protest, I grabbed the suitcase with the broken wheel. It was actually the heaviest of the bunch, but he didn't need to know that.

He rolled my other bag to the front door. "We're a few blocks away from the University. Just a short walk and you're there," he grunted trying to smile. "You're also near the Chernyshevskaya subway station."

The cream-colored building stood about ten stories tall. Leonid buzzed room 403.

A tinny voice over the intercom spoke in Russian. "Is this European University?"

Leonid leaned into the intercom. "Yes. We're here with the beautiful Ariel Garrison."

"Wait a minute," the voice said.

Leonid smiled at me. *Beautiful Ariel Garrison?* I wasn't sure how to take the compliment. School officials weren't supposed to say anything to students that sounded remotely like flirting, right? Maybe it was different in Russia.

In a few minutes, the door opened. Two men and one woman appeared, all young enough to be fresh out of college. Siblings, I guessed. The oldest brother wore a beard with a clean-shaven chin, making him resemble Hugh Jackman as the Wolverine comic book character. He greeted me in broken English.

"Hyello, we are host for you." The Hugh Jackman doppleganger shook my hand with a firm grip. My heart raced. I had always felt a connection with the Wolverine character: a loner, a man of secrets, living a life without ever letting love find a home inside his heart. This Wolverine look-a-like had model-stunning good looks. I wanted to feel that beard of his against my palm, my face. Hell, between my thighs. I suddenly wished Russian men had a ritual of greeting women by bending them over and fucking them silly. If I was going to live with this real life

Wolverine, it could lead to some tempting, dangerous liaisons.

He put his arm around the woman next to him. "I am Vlad. This is my wife, Inna."

Not his sister? Damn. Lucky gal.

Inna took my hand in both of hers and beamed. "Pleasure to meet." Her voice was sweet and sultry.

Vlad brought the youngest and tallest in front of him. "And this is our son, Pavel. We call him Pasha."

His son? They looked practically the same age.

Pasha stood confident, like a king, tall with broad shoulders. His clean-shaven face exposed a regal, square jaw and his scruff of tousled brown hair crowned his head. When he shook my hand, his hand held mine with a delicate touch. "Hyello."

I explained in Russian that I was good enough with the language to speak it. They didn't have to speak English.

"No." Vlad held up his hands. "We practice English. You help us speak."

I laughed. "Okay."

My time in Russia was going to be less lonely than I thought.

# CHAPTER 6

**M**Y ROOM was tiny, with just enough space for a double bed, a set of floor-to-ceiling shelves, a compact mocha desk, and a full-length mirror on the small closet door. I unpacked, placing my sweaters, jacket, and other clothes in the closet. I had prepared for two temperatures, cold and freezing. As I moved around the small room, the floorboards squeaked under me announcing their old age.

Inna poked her head into my room, smiled, and asked if I needed anything.

"A shower would be nice." I smiled back.

She showed me to the bathroom in the hallway. "Here is towel. Shower is on like this." She pulled a lever. "Hot," she turned on and off a knob. "Cold," she maneuvered another knob.

"Got it."

She held my arm gently and smiled, "Is okay?"

"Yes. Thank you."

"After, we eat. Okay?"

My first Russian dinner. "Good. I'm starving."

She left and closed the door. I wondered what dinner would be. Piroggi? Borsht soup? Beef stroganoff? I stripped off my wool sweater, T-shirt, jeans, bra, and panties. The hot water revived me from the long trip. I loved their soap. The suds smelled of chamomile.

When I got out of the shower, I ran a towel across my body to dry off.

I heard a floorboard squeak just outside the bathroom door. Was someone standing there?

"Hello?" I held still. "Does someone need to use the bathroom?"

No response.

I noticed the keyhole. Pasha could easily watch me through it. But would he be so bold? With his parents down the hall?

Boys will be boys. Thank goodness. I got a little thrill at being admired.

I shrugged my shoulders pretending to think no one was there.

Inna clanked dishes and pots in the kitchen, and from the sound of the TV blaring in the living room, Vlad was perhaps too busy watching TV to wonder what Pasha was doing.

Here it was, the first night of my stay, and already Pasha has seen me naked. I knew that eventually, some of the family members might accidentally see me naked, just not so soon. What also surprised me was that Pasha didn't strike me as a guy who would go out of his way to spy on naked women.

I went through my routine of drying myself off, but knowing Pasha watched me added excitement to each place I touched.

He saw me dry my thin arms. I got goosebumps along them.

He saw me dry my neck and shoulders. A heat flushed up to my face.

He saw me dry my petite breasts. A tingling tugged at my hardening nipples.

Oh, God, was that his breathing I heard?

He saw me dry my back and flat stomach. I felt butterflies.

He saw me dry my butt and between my legs. My budding cleft creamed for me not to move away from that spot.

He saw me dry my gorgeous legs, the best part of my body. My heart pounded knowing I probably turned him on with these legs.

He saw me dry my feet. My toes curled at the thought of him stroking his cock while he watched me dry my body.

His breathing became louder and ragged.

Drying myself didn't work. It just made me more

wet. Could that give me the excuse I needed to rub myself against the towel?

I fought my desire and put on my bikini panties. When I picked up my bra, I set it down again. Maybe I should wait until he's finished before getting dressed.

In just my bikini panties, I unzipped my makeup bag, leaned toward the mirror, and began putting on my eyeliner.

His breathing got louder.

In front of the small mirror, I stood with my back arched a little more than usual to make sure my pert breasts were as big as I could make them.

He grunted. Then the sound of heavy breathing stopped. I heard a zipper zip up.

He came. And I didn't get to see his facial expression of gratifying release. Maybe there was still time. What did his face look like after coming? Covering my boobs with my arm, I opened the door and peered out.

It wasn't Pasha who walked away from me down the hall. Pasha must have been the one watching TV. It was Vlad. My heart thumped knowing the Wolverine had just admired my body in the most intimate of ways.

He held a scrunched up handkerchief in his hand and said over his shoulder. "We eat now."

Then a heavy weight sunk in my gut. Was I a temptation for Vlad? What would Inna say? Would his lust for me interfere with his marriage? The last thing I wanted was to be the cause of breaking up a family. I decided I needed to call Leonid in the morning and have the university place me with a different family.

# CHAPTER 7

T HE KITCHEN had yellow cupboards and drawers matching the yellow walls. The dinner table stood out, a beautiful handcrafted piece with a curly vine design carved into the wooden legs.

I sat at the dinner table. Vlad sat across from me and didn't make any eye contact, which was fine with me. It would have been worse if he had winked at me and gave me a leering smile, as if to say he and I had a fun little secret to keep from his wife.

I brushed aside the nervous thought. My mouth watered at the anticipation of eating authentic Russian cuisine. Inna served us meat and potatoes, tasty and filling, but ordinary. Nothing like the foods often attributed to Russian culture. She sat beside Vlad and across from me and Pasha, who sat beside me. I relaxed my left hand on the table, and Pasha put his palm on the back of my hand. His gentle fingers triggered a whole damn electrical fire across my body. I wasn't expecting that. My skin had never responded to anyone's touch that way.

Uh, oh. Did he have a jealous girlfriend?

"You and me," he said. "We are the same. You are music major, yes?"

"Yes."

"*I* am music major. Even though we are both music majors, I see we have only one class together. Still, one is good, no?"

I liked his enthusiasm over spending time with me. "Yes. It is good."

He squeezed my hand gently. "I sit with you tomorrow."

Relief washed over me knowing at least one familiar face would be a part of my first day of school.

Pasha let go of my hand and had a bite of potatoes. "I listen to heavy metal. You like?"

"Yeah. Sometimes." Not my first choice.

"Tomorrow I take you to heavy metal band Kachat. They are super band."

"Will your girlfriend be there with us?"

Pasha laughed. "I am bachelor."

Wow. A guy as cute as him? Hard to believe.

He said, "We go to concert together. Just you and me, okay?

"Sure. Sounds like fun, actually."

Vlad took Inna's hand in his own and kissed it. In Russian, he thanked her for the delicious meal, then gave her a kiss on the lips. Their gaze lingered on each other. It didn't look like their marriage was in any danger. Vlad seemed genuinely in love with her, and she with him. I decided to wait a few days before telling my contacts at the university what had happened. I could wait before making the final decision of leaving this family.

I PREPARED FOR BED slipping into my thermal underwear, thinking about Vlad. I should have been upset with him for having the audacity to lust after me while his wife cooked in the kitchen. But I couldn't shake the excitement of such a delicious man wanting me. How often do you get to share a house with someone who looks like Hugh Jackman? Pasha didn't look so bad, either. Two gorgeous guys under the same roof.

I set my alarm for six a.m. and got under the covers. The blankets they provided me were heavy and warm. So nice.

What if Vlad had been the one to show me how the shower worked? I imagined him taking me by the hand and leading me into the bathroom.

I imagined him saying, "This lever turns water on and off."

In my fantasy, he demonstrated how to handle the lever with his firm grip. "This knob is for hot water. This one for cold water."

I smiled my thanks.

He put his hands to the top button of my blouse. "I help you get clothes off."

"I can undress myself."

He already tugged at the fourth button. "Is Russian custom."

Who was I to argue with custom?

I slipped deeper into my fantasy while I rubbed myself between my legs.

In my imagination, he slid my white blouse down off my arms and meticulously folded it, and rested it on the bathroom counter. He unbuttoned my jeans and unzipped them open, tugging them over my hips and down my legs. He did a double take and caressed the side of my thigh. "You have very nice legs."

"Thank you."

He placed his hands by one of my feet. "Lift."

I did and he pulled the pant leg off me.

"Lift." He did the same for the other pant leg. After folding it, he placed it on top of my blouse on the bathroom counter. "Turn around."

I turned, my back to him. I could feel his body close to mine. He placed his fingertips on my shoulders, tracing them as he nudged my bra straps off. With delicate fingers, he unclasped my bra, then caressed the sides of my arms as he slid the bra off me. I waited topless while I knew that behind me, he placed the bra atop my other clothes. Over my shoulder, I saw him kneel at my butt. He reached around my hips, and pushed his palms down the front of my panties. I felt his fingers slip through my curls. He glided his hands down the sides of my legs, taking my panties along with him. "Step."

I took a step forward out of the loops of my panties. When I faced him, he folded the panties and set them down.

He pulled off his shirt over his head revealing a sexy thatch of hair on his muscled chest.

This part of the fantasy got me breathing heavy in bed. I imagined his bare chest and dipped a finger inside myself.

Though I enjoyed the sight of his naked skin in my fantasy, I imagined being shocked by his actions and asked him, "What are you doing?"

He folded the shirt, set it alongside my clothes, and removed his shoes and socks. "I want make sure you do shower right. I stay and help."

I watched him unbuckle his pants, his chest rising and falling. His muscular arms bulged at the simple task of unzipping his pants. When he slid them off, I could see his thick, strong thighs under white briefs. A nice, big package bulged inside. After carefully folding his pants, he stripped off his briefs. His cock was a sight to behold. Already stiff and sticking straight out.

He tested the shower water until it was right, and held my hand to help me in.

He swiveled the soap between his hands working up a lather. "I soap you now. Turn."

I faced away from him and felt his soapy hands work into my shoulders. All the tension there melted away. I felt his cock rest in the valley of my butt. He reached around me and massaged my breasts, lathering them until my nipples shot jolts across my chest. There was still one place I ached for his touch. He slid his hand down my belly and found that one place.

I squirmed on his hand. "What about your wife?"

"My wife has physical condition. She no can have sex. Is seven years since I have sex. I help you with shower. You help me?"

To answer his question, in my fantasy, I faced him and got on my knees. His cock throbbed in my mouth. He moaned as I licked the underside. He groaned as I gently squeezed his sac. He called out my name as I took him inside my throat as deep as I could.

He helped me stand. "I fuck you now."

I hung a leg around his hip and guided him inside me. He kissed me. I felt his tip stretch me open wide, his body hot against my own. I felt his breath as he pushed deeper into me, his skin against my scorching nipples. I moaned. Was there anything that felt as good as this? I knew there wasn't. He began his thrusts, in and out, crashing into my body. He breathed with me. *In.* I clenched around his thickness. *Out.* My thighs trembled. *In.* I gasped at his length. *Out.* My heart pounded. He pumped into me faster. *Thrust.* I lost control over my body. *Thrust.* Crashes of waves shook me. *Thrust.* Only his arms kept me standing upright. *Thrust.* I shook. I quaked. I cried out.

My pussy quivered around my fingers and my body reduced down to shudders.

I relaxed in this bed, now initiated with my juices. I came three more times that night, each from a variation of the same fantasy. Each time there was some reason why it was okay for me to have sex with Inna's husband. In one, Vlad was actually Hugh Jackman, preparing for a movie role by doing research into what it was like to live with a Russian family. Inna wasn't really his wife so it was okay to play in the shower. A ridiculous possibility, but my fantasies aren't too particular when it comes to plausibility. My bed and dripping pussy could attest to that. Sleep came easily on my first night in this foreign land.

# CHAPTER 8

I N THE sunny morning, I stepped into the kitchen fully dressed in my jeans, T-shirt, and cardigan sweater. Pasha was sitting at the table eating leftovers from last night's dinner. Was the meat and potatoes we had a special dish prepared especially for me?

After our morning greetings, I opened some cabinets and drawers, working out how the kitchen was organized. I found the bowls and silverware easily. Pasha had showed me where they were the night before. "Where's the cereal?"

"Oh, sorry. Is in cabinet there." Pasha pointed to the corner cabinet.

I opened the cabinet and saw the cereals on the highest shelf. I could easily jump and get them, but showing off my powers grabbing cereal was not the best way to keep my skills a secret.

"Here. I help." He reached over my shoulder for the cereal. His body gently pressed against me from behind. My breathing hitched. As tall as he was, I knew he couldn't have reached the cereal without having his body come into contact with mine. He was simply helping me. Still, my body tingled at his warmth at my back. I wanted to lean into him.

He placed a hand on my shoulder and handed me a box of Corn Flakes, smiled and returned to his breakfast. Who knew that Corn Flakes could be so arousing?

We ate in silence. I glanced at him, he glanced at me. Of the two men in this family, he was the most dangerous liaison. While Vlad would never start a long-term relationship with me, Pasha had no attachments, no girlfriend, nothing to prevent himself from attempting to make me his girl. Attempting to kiss me. Attempting to get in my pants. I'd probably have to give him the "Let's just be friends" speech.

I played with the words. "Attempting" to make me his girl. "Attempting" to kiss me. "Attempting." "Tempting."

I chuckled.

"What is funny?" Pasha asked.

My mouth full of Corn Flakes, I mumbled, "Nothm."

He smiled. I tingled at the memory of him pressing up behind me.

I smiled back at him. *You're so cute when you're oblivious to how I'm picturing you rubbing your crotch against my backside.*

I'd nearly finished my cereal when Pasha placed his dishes in the sink.

He washed his hands and dried them on an orange dishtowel. "I get my books. You finish, and I walk you to university office. We get class schedule."

"Excellent. Thank you."

He left. I checked the time. Were we going to be late? Not sure how far the campus was, I decided to play it safe and rushed toward the sink. Playing it safe only made my goal of staying on time worse. My hurried jerking movements to the sink triggered the spoon to fall out of the bowl and onto the floor. The spoon's movement carried it under the refrigerator.

"Damn." I placed the bowl in the sink and dropped to the floor to peer under the fridge. The spoon's silhouette taunted me a few inches from my face. Though I tried to reach the spoon, my hand just didn't fit that far. I carefully lifted the fridge up a few inches with one hand and retrieved the spoon with the other.

"You finish breakfast? *Vot eto da!*"

I didn't turn around at Vlad's Russian version of "Holy cow." Instead I gently set the fridge down and faced him. Pasha stood beside Vlad. Vlad's jaw dropped in disbelief while Pasha seemed amused.

I stood, presenting them with the spoon. "I – uh – dropped the spoon." My cheeks burned and my stomach sank. Hopefully, I didn't completely make a mess of keeping my super strength a secret.

I dropped the spoon into the sink and the spoon clinked as it landed. "I'll get my bookbag, and we'll go, okay, Pasha?"

I brushed past them before he could answer.

A few minutes later, Pasha and I had our bags and were set to leave the apartment, I heard some grunts in the kitchen. Surely, Vlad wasn't playing with himself now? I peeked in and saw him on the floor with his hands at the base of the fridge, struggling and failing to lift it. I bit my lip to help choke down a laugh and caught up with Pasha who waited outside for me.

# CHAPTER 9

WE WALKED through the morning chill. I tucked a thumb under the strap of my backpack as Pasha escorted me to the campus. The streets were regular two-way lanes with apartment complexes lining the sidewalks. Not spectacular, but I knew the gorgeous bridges, buildings, and tributaries of the city were nearby in a different direction. I had plenty of time to see St. Petersburg's beauty another day.

Pasha moved at a brisk clip.

I quickened my pace to catch up and spoke. "If you don't mind me asking, how old are your parents?"

"My mother is thirty-one years old and my father is thirty-three years old."

That couldn't be right. "And how old are you?"

He smiled. "I am nineteen years old."

I did the calculation. Inna was twelve when she had Pasha? Pasha watched me with amusement. He must have known what I was thinking.

He adjusted the backpack on his shoulder. "Vlad and Inna adopted me. My first foster parents died. The Iltchenkos, my first foster parents, were friends with Vlad and Inna. One day, I was four years old, my parents and their friend Alex drank too much vodka. Alex drove them in a car fast. They crashed. Alex survived the crash, my parents did not."

My heart froze. "I'm so sorry. And the driver survived? You must hate him."

He shrugged. "Alex Mizin is in his own hell. He watches TV all day, he drinks, and he never leaves his house. But I am okay. I do not remember so good the Iltchenkos. Vlad and Inna? They are my family."

My heart poured out to him and I felt a connection. I considered telling him how I, too, lost a parent, but caught myself. Mentioning the loss of my dad would only lead to questions. Questions demanding answers I could never reveal.

"What about your real parents?" I asked.

He shrugged and didn't reply.

I changed the subject. "This is my last year in college. Yours too, right?"

"Yes. Why you are asking?"

"Do you have any plans after college?"

He grimaced. "I cannot leave Inna and Vlad.

They need me. I must stay."

"How come?"

"I must make sure they are okay."

"I hate to break it to you, but I'm pretty sure Vlad and Inna can take care of themselves. You should move on, explore the world, make music." I nudged him playfully.

He smiled but his grim demeanor quickly returned. "Perhaps you are right. Perhaps they are better without me."

Why did he look so sad about that? I decided it best not to press him.

We stepped into the Student Services office.

PASHA OFFERED to get our schedules from the office as I waited in the large, brightly lit hallway speckled with couches and bustling with other students. I sat on the brown leather couch across from the office.

People-watching was the sport of choice for the moment. Students lugged their backpacks over their shoulders, many of them guys dressed in skinny jeans and leather coats. I admit, my attention was also snared by a few girls who, as they hurried into the building, unzipped their long coats and revealed short skirts and low-cut tops.

A guy whose biggest bulge was his nose sat uncomfortably close to me on the couch. "*Privet*," he greeted me. He continued in Russian, asking if I wanted to have a good time.

I shrugged. "I don't speak Russian."

He nodded his understanding. "Americansky?"

"Yes."

He pursed his lips and scowled. I could practically smell the exhaust from his mental gears grinding.

"You want…?" He pressed his index finger into the flat palm of his other hand, the Russian hand-gesture for sex.

I laughed. Really? That's how he hits on girls? That pick-up strategy couldn't ever work, could it?

Pasha stepped out of the office. As soon as he saw the guy next to me making the sex gesture, Pasha strode to the couch, frowning. They had a brief exchange in Russian.

"Buzz off!" Pasha said in Russian and gestured with his hands the universal "go away" movement.

"You know her?" the nosy guy asked, continuing the Russian conversation.

"She's my girlfriend."

A thrill buzzed through me. I stifled a smile. Defeated, the young man stood and shuffled away.

Pasha sat beside me on the couch. He took a deep breath and spoke to me in English. "I am sorry for doing that, for saying I am boyfriend. I should not interrupt your chat with other men."

I put my hand around Pasha's firm bicep. "That was very gallant of you." Holy moly! His arm felt like solid muscle. Not huge, just tight.

"Gall…?"

"Gallant. Um…like brave or helpful."

"Oh. I am glad you like. Is not my decision who is your boyfriend. I thought maybe I make mistake. Maybe I – how you say – interfere?"

"In this case, I'm glad you interfered." I had become so used to taking care of myself, it was nice to have someone stand up for me.

"You do not need to be alone, Ariel."

My heart squeezed. Did he have any idea how much I wanted to believe him?

# CHAPTER 10

AT FOUR-THIRTY in the afternoon, I finished my first day of classes and sat on the couch outside the office to wait for Pasha. I had left my favorite pen in the History of Music classroom, but didn't want to rush back to the classroom and leave Pasha to wonder where I was. Best to wait for him first.

Earlier that day, just after lunch, Pasha and I had taken the History of Music class together. I was glad about that because I had a premonition History of Music was going to be a hard class. I could go to Pasha with help on memorizing the music, smoothing out the learning experience.

I traced my fingers along the leather seat of the couch. Where was Pasha? Most of the students had already gone for the day.

Having met the professors and the classmates, I buzzed with anticipation of the school year. The only class I didn't like was Counterpoint. The professor must have left his ability to enunciate at home, or maybe he had an ex-wife who won it in the divorce settlement. I couldn't understand a thing he had said.

I sat waiting. The hallway felt abandoned, but soon Pasha arrived. I greeted him with a quick hug. He gave me a nice, tight squeeze with his arms.

His chestnut brown eyes sparkled. "Sorry I am late. I talk to professor. He tell me story of his life. You have good day?"

"Very good. The only professor I had trouble with was Professor Adams in my Counterpoint class. I couldn't understand him."

"Professor Adams?" He laughed.

"What's so funny?"

"He is Americansky."

"He is? Well his Russian pronunciation sucks. Boy, if I have trouble understanding him, I can't imagine how hard it must be for native Russians to understand him."

"No one understand him." He motioned with his head. "Come. We go home now."

"Just a sec." I told him that I left my pen in the classroom. "I'll be right back."

At the History of Music classroom, I happened to open the door quietly. It was a good thing, too. Tanya, one of my classmates Pasha had introduced me to, was inside the room huffing with the professor. My jaw dropped. The way she was bent over the desk being prodded from behind by Professor Rasskazov, she was getting a good dose of physical ed. I closed the doorway enough to leave it open a crack for good visibility. I could not take my eyes away. They had already gone past the point of foreplay. He was pounding her hard and she stuffed a scarf in her mouth to keep from screaming.

I couldn't help it. The scene had me dripping.

She was going to get an A, no doubt about that. Did Svetlana the university rep think this was what I would stoop to for good grades? I would never do that.

Though by the ecstasy on Tanya's face, I had to admit it looked like fun.

She let loose an orgasmic scream through her scarf. My heart thumped in my chest, practically in time to the sound of the professor's slapping thrusts against her ass. He growled a low moan and pushed deep, keeping his cock buried to its hilt inside her. Thinking what it must have felt like to have his cum splash inside her made my nipples harden.

The two stilled, catching their breath. Tanya shuddered from the aftershocks of her climax. I closed the door quietly. As I walked away, a faint sound of laughter came from behind the door. I guess they realized someone was watching them. I just hoped they didn't know it was me. I'd be uncomfortable

talking to either one of them for the rest of the school
year.

# CHAPTER 11

REACHING Pasha outside the office, I sped past him. "Let's go."

"You have your pen?"

*Oh, geez. How do I answer him?* My ears burned hot even as we stepped outside into the cold.

"Ariel?"

I slid the straps of my book bag onto both shoulders and crammed my cold fists into my coat pockets. "I don't have it. It's still in the classroom."

It was his turn to catch up with my quick steps. "Why do you leave it there?"

I searched for a lie, but couldn't find any. There was no point in hiding it. Pasha would just pester me until I revealed the truth.

I stopped walking. "I saw something. In the

classroom."

Pasha raised his brows.

"When I went to go back for it, I saw Professor Rasskazov. And Tanya. They were…"

"Having sex?"

My cheeks flushed. "Yes."

He nodded. "They are boyfriend and girlfriend. For more than one year."

"They are?" I had to let that sink in. "Isn't that illegal?"

"No. The classroom is not best place, but it is not illegal for professor and student to have sex."

I shook my head. "I don't understand. It's illegal for professors to fraternize with their students in America. I thought it was illegal everywhere."

Pasha switched his backpack to his other shoulder and gestured for us to continue walking. "It *was* illegal. Before end of cold war. There were many laws. Too many laws."

"How can there be too many laws?"

"Before, people were taxed more than one hundred percent. How can you give more than one hundred percent?"

I knew a couple of American athletes who thought they could.

Pasha seemed a bit angry. "People will do the right thing if they are able to. But if you take more than one hundred percent of their money, how can they do the right thing? They can't. So the people, they cheated. They kept money hidden from government. They had to. Back then, the laws were strict. Too strict."

"Now it's better." I hugged my coat against the cold.

"Now it's not strict. After cold war, people were free. But they were too free."

"Too free?"

"Free to make slander. Free to drive drunk…" He shook his head with disapproval.

Drive drunk? Was he thinking about the man who killed his parents? Perhaps there was indeed such a thing as having too much freedom.

"Laws are coming back," Pasha said. "Drunk driving. It is now illegal again."

"That's good. But professors having sex with their students?"

He nodded. "That is still legal."

I thought about Tanya, the professor's girlfriend. "She wasn't doing it to get a good grade?"

"Tanya? No. She is smart girl. She does not need to have sex with professor to get good grade." He walked without saying anything further.

That was the day I started to rethink the difference between right and wrong. Culture shock began to set in.

# CHAPTER 12

**B**ACK at the apartment, I closed the door to my room. I wanted to get busy with homework before dinner. Pasha had said our evening plans to hear the band would not leave time for homework. I worked at changing into a studying mindset in my mental locker room, but after what I had seen my professor do to Tanya, my mindset had a different idea of what to wear in the mental locker room. First a red bikini, then lacy lingerie, then a plain white nightshirt with easy access to all my aching needs.

I caressed the seam on my jeans, remembering Tanya's stifled moans. If dating your professor wasn't considered wrong in this culture, what else wasn't considered wrong? A dripping part of me was very interested to study the answer to that question.

After washing my face with cold water, I did manage to apply myself to my homework. Pasha knocked on my door to give me a plate of chicken and potatoes. He said he didn't want me feeling hungry at the concert. I ate as I finished up a four-part Bach-style chorale for my Counterpoint class.

At seven-thirty, with my coat back on, I waved goodbye to Inna and Vlad. Pasha and I walked the streets to go see the heavy metal band Kachat perform. The word *kachat* meant "dance" or "sway," an appropriate name for a band. The evening air chilled colder than the afternoon but the sun was still up. It wouldn't set until after nine o'clock. The late night sun was another personality of Russia I had to get used to.

Pasha said, "The band is very good. The music is incredible. But the show, it is sexy. If you don't like, you tell me and we go home. Is no problem. Okay?"

I giggled. "Okay." It was cute how Pasha didn't want me to feel offended.

We strolled down Vosstaniya Street for over thirty minutes to the concert hall at Ligovsky Avenue. Pasha paid for me.

I followed Pasha into the dark hall that then dumped us into a wide concert hall. The noisy college-aged crowd prowled in leather, tattoos, piercings, and anticipation. A rich smell of pot filled the room. A stage graced the far end of the hall, and a dance floor took up most of the space. The lights dimmed low. The audience cheered. Darkness consumed the room. I couldn't see exactly what was going on up front.

The stage lights popped on. A solid hunk of man with a shaved head posed center stage in front of a standing microphone. The room hushed.

In a burst of noise, walls of thrumming sound from guitar chords shook the room. A pounding steady drum rhythm hammered inside my chest. The strapping muscle man sang and I practically creamed my jeans right there. While the audience in front of me danced, I stood still. I was too engrossed by the undulations of the singer and how he had managed to enter my body by just using the sound of his voice.

"You like?" Pasha moved his head in time with the music.

Distracted by the sensations, I could barely nod.

The music crashed and pounded the way I expected, but it wasn't the same three chords over and over like most heavy metal music. This band actually had sophistication to their songs. No wonder Pasha, a fellow music major, admired them.

While most of the young people in the audience had piercings and tattoos. One guy sported a Mohawk and a swastika tattooed on the back of his neck.

I pointed him out to Pasha. "Is he a neo-Nazi?"

He shook his head. "No. Is not hatred. Is ignorance. Is fad."

I glanced around at the billowing bodies and spotted three others with swastika tattoos. A sick feeling bubbled in my stomach, but those guys didn't know the history behind the swastika, I kept telling myself. I hoped that was true.

As the next song began, two thin women came from either side of the stage and danced, stripping of their clothes slowly. The guys in the crowd roared. By the end of the song, those girls were bare naked. The break between songs lingered longer than usual. The stage lights flickered. The crowd cheered. For flickering stage lights? There had to be some other reason they cheered. As if they knew what was coming next.

Then the audience chanted, "Kar-lik! Kar-lik! Kar-lik!"

A naked woman, barely three feet tall, came on stage, prouder than a peacock with gilded feathers. I don't think I've ever heard a crowd cheer as much as this audience did. Karlik, Russian for "dwarf," that must have been her stage name.

The next song started and "Karlik" strutted with her tiny legs and tiny hips over to the singer. Though most of her body was small, her boobs were bigger than mine. As he growled out the verse, Karlik stood by his side, and slowly began to unzip his fly. Only by the audience's enthusiastic urging did she bring that zipper all the way down. The singer kept on singing and ignored what she was doing.

I glanced at Pasha. He had his eyes closed and bobbed his head in time to the music with a huge smile on his face.

Karlik gave a look to the crowd and gestured as if to say, "Shall I take it out?"

The audience cheered.

She buried her hand inside his pants. I could see by the bulge swimming in the front of his jeans that she had to move her hand a bit to get a firm grip on him.

Finally she pulled it out and the singer kept right on singing. My god, the thing practically came to his knees! The cheers overpowered the music when she worked her little hands along his length. The contrast of the size of her hands made his cock look like a baseball bat. I swallowed and wondered what it would be like to have that much man inside me. My nipples hardened applauding my fantasy.

Karlik faced the audience and pointed to her mouth with a questioning expression.

Applause, hoots, and whistles filled the room. "Oh, yes," the applause seemed to say. "Suck his dick."

The singer turned showing off his profile. Karlik stuffed that thing in her mouth. She took him to the back of her throat, and down further, and further. That Karlik was a talented woman. I imagined how exquisite that must have felt for the singer. Heat flooded my chest. As impressive as Karlik was, I had to give the singer credit for being so able to stay focused on his singing while she swallowed him down.

The singer groaned. So much for staying focused. The crowd laughed. She popped his slick, shiny cock from her lips, and he wailed the final notes to the song.

I found myself applauding and hooting with the rest of them. Pasha and I shared a smile and my heart pounded with the excitement of what the next song would be like.

The next song was a brilliant five-four meter. The crowd's screams practically burst through my eardrums when the song started to play.

The singer sang the first verse. The short woman rubbed the backside of her body against his legs. I swayed to the unique rhythm. One-two-three-four-five, one-two-three-four-five.

The singer picked up Karlik and everyone went wild. He turned her so that she faced us and placed his cock between her legs, slowly impaling her. Her face showed a genuine ecstasy. This was one part of the show she was not performing. God, my panties were soaked. I squirmed along to the pounding music.

The singer had a specific rhythm to the way he fucked her. He thrust hard twice, then pushed slowly for three counts. Thrust, thrust, push-two-three. Thrust, thrust, push-two-three. Now I understood the band's name. *Kachat* didn't just mean "dance" and "sway," it was also the Russian word for "ride" and "pump."

Suddenly I noticed how quiet the crowd was. I looked around. Several of the guys in the audience were fucking their girlfriends from behind. At least I suspected those girls were their girlfriends. For all I knew they may be having sex with strangers. The guys were matching the singer's rhythm.

Thrust, thrust, push-two-three. Thrust, thrust, push-two-three.

The singer's voice wavered as he belted out the lyrics and pummeled the small woman simultaneously. Someone behind me ground his crotch against my ass. I imagined it was an invitation for me to bend over and join the choir. Before I had a chance to grab him by the balls and squeeze him into leaving me alone, Pasha shoved the guy away and said in Russian, "Fuck off!"

Pasha put his arm around my waist. "I do this so no one else try fuck you. They will think you are with me."

Our sides were touching as we watched the small woman holding herself up by grabbing on to the singer's cock between her legs. Tingles coursed through me at this shared view, feeling Pasha's warm body beside me. Watching this together felt like I crossed an intimate boundary with my housemate.

Thrust, thrust, push-two-three. Thrust, thrust, push-two-three.

The unique five-four rhythm captured me in ways

I knew affected me more as a musician than it might others. Pasha was also a musician. It must have made a similar impression on him. I could even feel our breaths inhaling and exhaling together. My nipples sought out to be squeezed. The singer's voice vibrated deep in my chest.

Pasha's hand glided down from my side to my ass. I kept myself from grinning at the cute way he made his move on me.

I delicately repositioned his hand up around my waist, and just to show there were no hard feelings, I put my arm around his waist.

The song went into an instrumental. The singer took this opportunity to put on a full show. He had an arm wrapped below her neck to keep her shoulders against his own. His other hand held the microphone at her lips. When he started jumping, my jaw dropped. She yelped with each hop, holding onto the cock between her legs as if she were trying to prevent him from penetrating her further and further. But that wasn't pain on her face, that was near climax.

I was dripping buckets. I wanted to rub myself, I wanted someone inside me, I wanted to grab Pasha's crotch but managed to keep my desires in check. The way the music kept going and going without any singing, I realized the music wasn't playing the instrumental, it was playing an improvised cadenza, playing on and on until the climax.

No, not the climax. *His* climax.

He jumped in time with the eighth notes, then faster, little hops with the sixteenth notes. The small woman huffed out her staccato cries of bliss.

My breathing matched Pasha's. I held him close to my side and together we swayed to the music. My eyes stayed riveted on the stage. My body ached to be touched. I wanted Pasha to squeeze my breasts, knead them in time to the music

The singer screamed his orgasm. He pulled her off his cock and set her down on the stage. She grabbed his length in front of her face and stroked it, pumping out jets of white all over her face and tits.

I clenched my thighs, imagining it was me feeling the singer's spray and looking up into the face of the singer. No, not the singer's face. Pasha's face flashed in my mind. Pasha's face of ecstasy and release.

The audience belted out their enthusiastic clamor. The music exploded in a finale of incredible crescendo.

The song ended, but the cheers kept the concert hall reverberating with deafening sound. Some couples were still fucking. Having missed the cue to climax with the singer, the guys were pumping fast to fill their girls with cum.

"You like?" Pasha squeezed my waist.

I exhaled. "That was something, alright."

"Now comes finale."

"You mean that wasn't it?"

The band started their next song, but it moved

slower than the others. Low notes moaned out a seductive waltz. The two tall, thin dancers moved with sensual, sultry motions to the front of the stage. I realized by the unusually slow rhythm this wasn't the climax of their show. It was the last song. The cuddling after sex. How sweet.

As the singer sang the end of the second verse, the crowd got louder and put up their arms. A cymbal crash, then the singer began the chorus. The two girls at the edge of the stage collapsed flat upon the hands of the crowd.

My heart thumped. I watched astonished and captivated as the two girls let their bodies ride the sea of hands, fingers touching them everywhere.

I thought *my* promiscuous behavior was extreme. But letting your body get groped by all these guys? All at once? These two girls surfing weren't risking pregnancy, but I wasn't sure how safe it was to have all those strangers' fingers inserted in their pussies and up their asses.

One of the girls was coming close to us. She was face down, hands and fingers stroking her legs, supporting her belly, squeezing her breasts, stroking her hair. It must have felt so good.

She reached us. Her eyes were closed, a big smile of bliss on her face. I let go of Pasha and reached up to let my hand glide down the front of her shoulder to her breast and across her nipple. She opened her eyes, saw my face, and smiled like she knew a secret. Like she knew I had never touched a girl like that before. And she was right. Then she was gone behind us.

Pasha squeezed his arm around my waist.

I scowled. "Why didn't you touch her?"

He shrugged. "I don't like."

What was that supposed to mean? Was he gay? That couldn't be it. After all, he put his hand on my ass. Maybe he had high ideas of what was right and what was wrong. Or could he be a virgin? Saving himself? That seemed unlikely. Especially a guy as attractive as he was.

The crowd caressed and fingered the two girls all the way back to the stage. The girls stood, and shimmied and danced on stage to the end of the slow, raucous song.

I applauded along with the audience. Lots of people yelled to show their love of the performance. I squinted against the sudden bright lights illuminating the auditorium. People headed toward the exits.

I felt Pasha's arm still around my waist. "You can let go now."

"You want I let go?"

I nodded.

He removed his arm. I nearly collapsed and had to grab on to Pasha's shirtsleeve. He laughed. My legs wobbled. Had he been holding me up this whole time?

He grabbed me around the waist again and chuckled. "Come. We drink now."

# CHAPTER 13

W E WENT to a nearby bar. The place reeked of cigarettes as if we had just entered a smoker's lung. Pasha led me to a table where two young men sat smoking cigarettes and drinking beers. In English, Pasha introduced his friends to me, Danny and Sergei. Pasha turned a chair backwards at his friends' table and sat straddling the back of the chair.

Pasha put his arm around my shoulder as if we were buddies and said to his friends, "She is Americansky. Practice your English with her."

Sergei shoved a strand of his blonde hair from in front of his eyes. "You have boyfriend?"

"No," I said.

Pasha tugged the collar on Sergei's burgundy button-up shirt and continued the English conversation. "Ask her where she is from."

"Where do you come from?"

"Kansas," I said.

Pasha laughed. "Where are you really from?"

I had no idea what Pasha was getting at. From the looks on the faces of Danny and Sergei, neither did they. "Kansas?"

Pasha chuckled. "She is funny."

Danny tapped some ash from his cigarette into an ashtray. He hadn't said anything, so I decided to include him. "How do you know Pasha?"

Danny's brown eyes darted at Sergei. "Uh." Did he understand English? "We met at restaurant."

He understood English well enough. By the way he couldn't make eye-contact with me, he probably just wasn't used to talking to girls.

Pasha whacked Danny's arm with the back of his hand. A friendly looking gesture, but Danny winced and rubbed his arm.

Pasha said to me, "Danny and Sergei and me are business partners."

"Business partners?"

"I have a truck." Pasha shrugged. "Danny and Sergei hire me to drive expensive package to restaurant."

"Ah, I see." Would it be too sensitive to ask what kind of packages?

"I buy us beer." Pasha climbed off the chair as if he were getting off a horse.

"No thanks, I don't drink alcohol," I said.

Pasha's eyes widened. "Why you come to Russia?"

I tucked a loose lock of my hair behind my ear. "There are puh-lenty of other countries that drink, you know. Yours is not the only one with the privilege."

He shrugged. "Okay. I get vodka, then. Just for me." He walked away.

I turned to Danny and Sergei expecting their full attention on me, the pretty foreigner. Instead, they spoke to each other in Russian. I eavesdropped.

Sergei blew out a puff of smoke and spoke softly to Danny who was nursing both a beer and a cigarette. "When we first enter the store, you've got to be confident. Always point your gun at the cashier's face. Scare him. Otherwise, he'll never hand over the cash."

Danny motioned with subtle jerks of his head at me.

"Don't worry." Sergei leaned back in his chair and peered at me. "The American idiot doesn't understand a word we're saying."

I pasted on a goofy grin and spoke in English doing what I could to sound like an airhead. "What are you guys talking about?"

Sergei dismissed any worry with a wave of his hand. "Is nothing. Just business. Is boring."

Danny finished his cigarette and peeled the label

off his beer bottle. In Russian, he continued his conversation with Sergei. "How much time will we have to escape?"

"From the time we leave the store, the cashier will probably call the police. That will give us at least seven minutes to get to Pasha's truck and escape. Plenty of time."

"I'd still feel better if Pasha knew what we were really doing."

"Trust me. The less he knows, the better." Sergei rolled up his sleeves. I sucked in a breath. A tattoo of a sickle cutting two arrows, the same symbol that had been branded on my father's forehead, peeked out. "Pasha's the kind of guy who won't do anything against the law. Even if it's in his best interest."

Danny nodded. I examined Danny's skin, and there it was, just above his wrist, the same tattoo. A shard of ice sliced down my spine. I shivered.

A voice said, "What is it I miss?"

Shit. It was Pasha holding a large bottle of vodka. If he gave away that I spoke and understood Russian, his "friends" might be compelled to silence us.

I grabbed Danny's hand and placed my other hand on his wrist. "So Danny, you said you met Pasha at a restaurant?"

"Yes." Since he wasn't exactly the alpha male of this crew, I knew he was the easiest guy to innocently interrogate.

"Which restaurant is it?" I flashed a flirtatious

smile at him.

"Tkemali at Vladimirskaya."

"Hey, Danny!" Sergei nudged his friend's shoulder and spoke in English. "I think she like you."

I ignored him and batted my eyelashes at Danny. "If you go to the restaurant so often, you must work there. Are you a waiter or a chef?"

"Waiter."

There it was. The change in pulse, the eyes shifting away, but most important was the slight biting of his lip. I knew he was lying. His lip bite was the tell. I had successfully set the baseline for determining when he was lying and when he was telling the truth.

"Did you also meet Sergei at the restaurant?" I asked.

"Yes." No shifting of the eyes or biting of the lip.

The truth.

"Do you like Sergei?"

"Of course. He is my friend." His eyes shifted right, then left, the lip bite.

A lie.

I had to stay in character. "Do you like me?"

He blushed. Pasha and Sergei laughed.

I squeezed Danny's hand. "You like me, don't you, Danny?"

"Yes." His pulse quickened, his eyes shifted away, but he didn't bite his lip.

The truth.

"I like you, too. I think you're sexy."

The other guys whooped and howled.

"Does your boss pay you well?"

"Yes."

The truth.

Pasha said in Russian to Sergei, "Women. They always want rich men."

Danny laughed.

I squeezed Danny's hand again to keep his focus on me. "Is your boss a nice man?"

"Yes."

A lie.

"Is he a powerful man?"

"Very powerful."

The truth. I may have figured out where the man who had my father tortured could be found.

"Does your boss run a lot of dangerous operations?"

"What?" Danny scowled.

Sergei scrutinized me. Shit.

I smiled. "If you're the kind of guy who does some dangerous things, I have this weakness. I always want to have sex with brave guys who do dangerous things."

"I do a lot of dangerous things." Danny told the truth.

"So do I," Sergei chimed in and smirked.

"Okay, okay." Pasha separated my hands from Danny's "Is enough."

I overdramatized a pout, then winked at Danny. He smiled.

The night chased to a half past midnight. To my amazement, Pasha drank four entire bottles of vodka and still didn't seem wasted.

"He is best drinker in all of St. Petersburg," Sergei explained puffing on another cigarette. "Pasha can drink more than anyone without going to sleep."

By the time Danny and Sergei left, I was fortunate to have kept under wraps that I spoke Russian and that I'd heard their plans to rob a store.

Pasha may not have passed out at the bar, but I still had to hold him up as we walked the six blocks home. After the way he stood up for me on campus and at the concert, protecting me from undesirable men, I felt good about getting the chance to return the favor by taking care of him.

"Ariel. Beautiful Ariel. You and me, we are the same." Pasha held up a finger. "I thought I was only one. But you are one, too." He shook his head and held up two fingers. "Not one-two. One, too. T-o-o-o." He spelled the word. "Wait. That too many 'O's." His two fingers came up higher. "Not two many. Too many. Ha, ha. 'Two many.' I am funny. You like joke?"

I giggled. "Yes. You're a very funny guy." His drunk talk amused me.

"You, too. You are funny. 'Kansas.' Ha, ha." He spoke in a high falsetto voice to mimic my own. " 'I am Ariel. I am from Kansas.' Ha, ha."

I shook him. "Hey. Are you making fun of me?"

"No! I never make fun. I love you."

I felt the heat of a blush rise up to my face unbidden. Just drunk talk, I convinced myself.

He whispered. "You like Kachat?"

He might have been asking if I liked to dance and sway. A dripping part of me hoped he was asking if liked to ride and pump. "You mean tonight's heavy metal band? Kachat? Yeah, they were very talented."

"You have wet panties. You are horny? I am horny. You want to fuck?"

How did he know my panties were wet? I must have been careless with keeping my legs crossed when sitting down in the bar. "I don't think that's a great idea, Pasha. What if your parents found out?"

He nodded, licking his lips. "Yes. You are right. We must keep us a secret."

He was the first man who ever described our relationship as an "us." I choked down an unexpected sob. Just hearing that word used that way made me realize how much I had longed for such intimacy. How much I wanted for there to be an "us" with some man. Especially a man like Pasha. But that could never be.

I could never put Pasha, or any man, in such jeopardy.

# CHAPTER 14

WHEN we got back to the apartment building, I balanced the inebriated Pasha against my shoulder as I helped him upstairs. Inside the apartment, I noticed the coat rack was bare. Inna and Vlad must not have been home. I was relieved to know I wouldn't wake them.

I helped Pasha to his room and placed him on his bed. He bent over and struggled to untie his shoelace.

I shook my head. "Leave your shoes on and just go to sleep."

"I can't sleep with clothes on." He smiled at me. It was a cute lopsided drunk smile.

I rolled my eyes, but felt a little naughty thrill tingle through me. "Hold still."

His knotted laces were super tight and took a little more dexterity and strength than I normally used. Without breaking anything, I tugged off his socks and shoes.

"Now the rest of my clothes." His smile was a little too wide.

I hauled off his jacket.

"Lift your arms," I said.

When he did, I yanked up his sweater and t-shirt. Wow! He was in great shape. As he leaned back on his pillow, arms crossed under his head, he smiled at me sleepily. I admired how just that small movement made his biceps bulge and his abs ripple.

I stood with my hands on my hips. "Okay?"

"Can't sleep with pants on." His jeans hugged his slim hips.

Boy, was I really going to do this? Though I didn't have a clear baseline of when Pasha was lying or telling the truth, he was probably lying. He could sleep just fine with his pants on. But I was still hot as hell, and as soon as I got to bed, I knew my fingers would get a good exercise. I also knew that helping out Pasha would also help my fingers get closer to their goal by giving me a good picture to focus on: taking off Pasha's pants.

*Okay, internal video camera. Start recording for later.*

I got down on my knees beside his bed and unbuttoned his pants. He watched me with a riveted gaze, his chest rising and falling with deep breaths. I unzipped his fly and grabbed hold of the sides of the jeans' waistline. When he lifted his waist, I tugged them down to his thighs.

The bulge inside his boxer briefs looked inviting tucked in there. My breathing got heavier.

I peeled his pants off his muscular legs and stood up, drinking in his entire body with my hungry gaze. My nipples hardened. My pussy clenched. I needed something inside. And quick.

"Goodnight," I said but I didn't move. Translation: Grab me and pull me down to your bed. Fuck me hard. Be the one who takes me, so that I know I'm not taking advantage of you.

He turned over on his side, showing his great backside to me. "Goodnight."

I stood still. What was I waiting for? My gaze fell on an envelope that lay on his bedside table. The stamped and addressed envelope, ready to be mailed, was addressed to Alex Mizin. Wasn't that the guy who drove drunk and got Pasha's foster parents killed? I hoped Pasha hadn't written a hate letter. Though it was none of my business, I delicately removed the letter from the unsealed envelope and read what Pasha had written.

My heart poured out as I read the words. I beamed with admiration. My whole opinion of Pasha changed. He needed to mail this letter. I just hoped he'd get the courage to do so.

I tucked the letter into its envelope and returned it to Pasha's bedside table. I tiptoed out of his room to let the remarkable man sleep.

***

Back in my bedroom, I stripped as fast as possible and slipped under the covers. My thermal underwear could wait. I pictured Pasha's amazing body as my fingers frantically danced between my legs.

The sound of the front door opened. Vlad's baritone voice bellowed laughter. In slurred Russian I was able to hear him say to Inna, "Let's fuck."

"I'm tired, Vlad."

I couldn't be sure at Vlad's response, but it sounded like, "Fine. I'll fuck someone else then."

But that couldn't have been what he said because Inna said, "Ariel is in bed." Clearly telling him to be quiet because I was trying to sleep. "Be gentle."

"Okay. Don't wake up trouble while it sleeps quietly." He chuckled.

I heard a few bumps and doors opening and closing. I tried to return to my fantasy of Pasha, but the house sounds scattered my focus.

A moment later, my door opened. Vlad stood in the doorway, highlighted by the hallway light. I turned away onto my side. The sound of his footsteps squeaked along the floorboards. He was getting closer.

"You are such a beautiful lady." Vlad still spoke in Russian, his pronunciation slurred by drink.

I heard him unbuckling his pants, a zipper unzipping, clothes swishing off skin, a drunken stumble. An entire percussion section drummed inside my chest. Was he really going to get in bed with me? That was so wrong.

So why wasn't I stopping him?

The covers lifted, cold air slipping along my back. His warm body came in contact with mine. I stiffened, eager to feel the body of the Wolverine fill me, frightened at the thought of betraying Inna's trust and having unprotected sex. My heart drummed a rolling thunder in my chest.

He stroked my arms, his voice and chest rumbling against me in Russian. "So soft. So beautiful. Your arms are like porcelain."

I felt him growing hard along my ass. *Ariel is in bed. Be gentle.* Could it be that Inna suggested this to him? That getting in my bed wouldn't bother her?

As impossible as it was, I wanted to believe it because I wanted him. God, I wanted Vlad so much. And as long as I pretended to be asleep, this would be all Vlad's doing. It wouldn't be my fault. I wouldn't be betraying Inna. And since Vlad and I couldn't ever have a committed relationship, I would never be putting his life in danger. Just a night of grinding against each other without penetration. Just this one time.

I tilted my hips to feel his length against me, desire dripping out of me.

Vlad reached over me and grabbed my breast, gliding his fingers across my nipple. Electricity sparked through me, curling my toes.

"I'm going to fill you with my cock and explode inside of you."

He humped the crevice of my butt. I slid my hand between my legs to add to my pleasure. The buzz I got made me dizzy.

He grunted. "You're so sexy. You're so…"

He stopped moving. What was happening? Why did he stop? Then I heard a snore.

Terrific. Neither of us had the chance to climax. I couldn't wait any longer. I rubbed frantically, squirming on my fingers. I ground my hips against him. This wasn't wrong, was it? He came to my room. He wanted this first, not me.

I reached behind me and felt his long length. He had a thin one. I knew just what would send me over the edge. Caution and morality lost their place in my dictionary. I needed release.

With his cock in my hand, I guided it at the entrance of my ass. I was pretty certain that just pushing the tip around the edge was safer than putting it in my pussy.

I relished the sensation of him behind me. Dramatic sweeps of music played along my skin.

I was with Vlad. With Hugh Jackman. With Wolverine, the loner. The one who understands me more than anyone ever could. His cock in my hand.

I fiddled two fingers in and out of my channel. My fingering struck all the right chords. I moaned, wanting more.

I pushed his tip inside, my ass clenching him.

Like the rising crescendo of the heavy metal band, my body's muscles felt waves of a finale rising higher and higher. And at the peak, that highest and loudest series of notes, I stifled a cry, squeezed my breasts, and pushed myself down on his cock until he was all the way inside me. I shuddered and shook.

When my body finished its convulsions, I lay still. The remaining overtones of my orgasm still rang, my rim pulsing around Vlad in time to the throbbing between my legs. I placed a hand on my clit and gently soothed her to peace.

But as the world of right and wrong, action and consequence, came crashing down on me, I wondered, what had I done?

I carefully slid up off Vlad, his member still solid as ever.

He'd come into my room to take advantage of me, and instead I'd taken advantage of him. And poor Inna. There was no denying it, I'd completely betrayed her trust.

"Sorry, gorgeous," I whispered. I pushed my back against Vlad, and kept pushing so that he fell off the bed. He hit the floor with a thud. I hoped I didn't hurt him.

"What?" He groaned in Russian. There was silence. Then he snored.

Good. He didn't seem hurt by that little fall.

Maybe when he woke up, he wouldn't remember any of what had happened tonight.

# *CHAPTER 15*

T HE following week at the university, we had a pop quiz in Music History. I wasn't sure I'd do well because we had gone over a lot of information. The quiz would be a breeze for Tanya. I knew that for certain. Not because she was the professor's girlfriend, but because over the past few days, I'd noticed she was the brightest student in the class. I knew by the way she always put her hand up to answer the questions the professor asked, and by the way she always got the answers correct. Either she already knew the curriculum or she did a ton of studying.

Professor Rasskazov handed out the quiz and told us we had ten minutes to finish.

I scanned the test. There were ten fill-in-the-blank questions, and ten minutes was plenty of time to complete the quiz. If you knew the material.

What happened next surprised me. Everyone got out of their seats and started discussing the answers. Most of them were looking over Tanya's shoulder.

One classmate peeked at what I had written, so I pulled my paper away. "Hey!" Wasn't that cheating?

The professor sat at his desk and raised his eyebrows at me as if to ask if I had a problem. I couldn't believe it. He must have been known across campus as the professor who lets his students cheat.

Then I realized the real meaning behind what the University foreign exchange student reps had said to me on the day I arrived. *We'd be surprised if you didn't get good grades.* They weren't thinking I'd have sex with a professor to get good grades. They were referring to the cheating. At least, in the US it would be cheating. Here in Russia, getting the answers from someone else seemed like regular classroom behavior.

I finished the quiz and looked at my answers.

"Brahms, not Berlioz." The low voice behind me was accompanied by a gentle hand on my shoulder. I looked up from my seat. Pasha. "Number seven."

Question number seven asked which composer wrote *La Damnation de Faust.* I had written Berlioz as my answer. "You don't think it's cheating to give away the answers?"

He shrugged. "I could be wrong. Maybe you are right and it is Berlioz."

He spoke the truth. All my classmates could tell me what they thought was the correct answer, but I still had to rely on my own knowledge to make the right choice. Ultimately, what was right and what was wrong was my decision. I read the question again. The more I thought about it, the more I realized I had mixed up Brahms's *La Damnation de Faust* with Berlioz's *Tragic Overture*. Pasha was right. It *was* Brahms. Not Berlioz.

# CHAPTER 16

A T HOME that night, I lay on the floor of my room completing the homework for Orchestration class. I didn't bother taking off my shoes. I knew I'd still need them.

There was a knock on my bedroom door.

"Come in."

Pasha poked his head in. "I go now to help friends."

I pretended to be distracted by my homework. "Have fun."

As soon as he closed the door, I sprung from the floor and put on my coat. It was going to be cold with the combination of the outdoor temperature and wind-chill factor. I heard the front door open and shut. Hopefully, Pasha wouldn't be quick to start his truck and leave.

I opened the window and jumped down from the fourth floor to the sidewalk. Pasha sat already in his truck, pulling away from the curb. Making sure he wouldn't see me in his rear-view mirror, I kept my head low as I ran after him. He sped to about thirty miles per hour.

I ran faster and caught up with him just long enough to jump onto the flatbed of the truck. I lay down on my belly as he drove to the main street. The wind swiped across me on the flatbed. I had full appreciation for my jacket, even though my body still chilled to a freezing cold temperature.

Some ten minutes later he slowed down and turned off the main street. I wiggled my numb fingers and toes to get the warm blood circulating. Soon after, he pulled over. Keeping my head down I heard him speaking in Russian to some young men. I recognized the voices. He was speaking to Sergei and Danny.

"Where to?" Pasha sounded cheerful.

"I'll give you directions. Danny, get in." Sergei was running the show, like I expected.

As the truck pulled away from the curb, I peeked out and saw Tkemali, the restaurant Danny had mentioned from the night before. Their home base.

What was I going to do? Use my sexual prowess to convince them not to go through with the robbery? Not very smart of me, going without a plan.

I didn't have any danger of being seen until we stopped again. Twenty minutes later, Pasha stopped in a brighter part of the city, an area where the shops still had business this late in the evening. Very bad. The lights would give me away as soon as they got out of the truck. I jumped off the back and crawled underneath the truck.

The truck doors opened and closed. Their feet stepped inches away from my face.

Sergei spoke in Russian. "Stay right here, Pasha. We'll be back in about twenty minutes."

"No problem. I just need to take a piss in the bushes."

"You'll be right back?"

"Sergei, come on. It doesn't take me twenty minutes to take a piss."

Two pairs of feet ran off while the last pair, Pasha, walked away.

What were my choices? I could run and use my strength to stop Sergei and Danny from committing the crime. But what if they change their mind on their own? Not likely, but I didn't feel right pre-empting an attack. Anything to physically stop Sergei and Danny would compromise my identity, and Pasha would discover my super abilities. Revealing my secret would lead to questions, then rumors, then government intervention. It would put Pasha and his family in danger. I wasn't going to do that.

I saw Pasha's feet walking back to the truck, so I

climbed out from underneath.

"Ariel! What you are doing here?" He smiled brightly at me, seeming pleasantly surprised.

"Pasha, we have to leave. Sergei and Danny are robbing the store, and they're making you their getaway driver."

"Sergei? And Danny? They are not like that. They are friends."

"They are not your friends. They are just using you and your truck. Please. We have to leave right now."

He scowled and shook his head. "I talk to them."

I had to physically push against his chest to stop him walking towards the store. "Pasha, you can't. They might kill you."

"Death does not scare me." He kept on walking. What the hell? Was he suicidal?

I grabbed his arm. "Trust me. Please, Pasha. Let's just drive away." He let me tug his arm and lead him back to the truck. His smirk suggested that he found my physical handling of him amusing.

An alarm rang into the night. The door to the store opened. Sergei and Danny sped toward us, glancing over their shoulder.

I grabbed on tighter to Pasha's arm. "Quick. Let's hide under the truck. Please, Pasha. Trust me."

He scowled, reassessing the situation. Then nodded. He scooted under the truck, face up. I lay beside him on the cold blacktop.

If Sergei or Danny looked underneath the truck on my side, I could easily kick them or punch them in the face. The trouble was, if they looked underneath on Pasha's side, Pasha would be in trouble, and I'd have no way to kick or punch that side.

"I have to cover all sides," I muttered.

"What?"

I ignored Pasha's question and climbed on top of him, chest to chest, face to face. Even though the truck was high off the ground, it was a tight squeeze. At least I now had him fully protected. He scowled, but didn't object. Pasha's breathing got heavier. The ambient light from the street lamps revealed him looking into my eyes seemingly unafraid.

Sergei's and Danny's racing feet stopped beside the truck. They dumped their stolen goods onto the back of the truck. By the way the back of the truck weighed down onto my ankles, whatever they stole must have been heavy. By spreading my legs over Pasha's, my ankles no longer felt the truck on top of them.

"Where the hell is Pasha?" Danny said in Russian, sounding scared.

"I don't know. I could have sworn I saw him just a moment ago."

"Do you think he's still taking a piss?"

"Maybe," Sergei said. "Get in the truck."

The doors opened and closed. Their weight pressed me harder against Pasha. My breasts crushed into his chest. I could feel him getting hard against my waist. How could he be aroused at a time like this?

When I had first met Sergei and Danny at the bar, they had said that they'd have seven minutes before the police would arrive to respond to the alarm. I had to make sure Sergei and Danny didn't find us before then.

Pasha stroked my hair. "You are so beautiful."

I didn't understand. Why wasn't he worried about getting caught? He'd said he didn't fear death. I remembered a friend who seemed to come out of a deep depression being cheerful and giving away her things. When she committed suicide, I realized her cheerful nature came from thinking she found the solution to all her problems: death. If Pasha had suicidal thoughts recently, then yes, he would have no reason to fear death. For him to kill himself? That would be a waste of such a handsome, kind man.

He kept right on peering into my eyes. We synched our flow of breaths to breathe easier. When I breathed out, he breathed in. I breathed in, he breathed out. I admired the way a lock of his dark hair curled over his forehead and the way his jawline was square and strong. He was such a good-looking guy. I decided to give him something to live for and kissed him. My intention was to just lift his spirits with that kiss, but it didn't quite work out as I'd planned. His kiss in return was powerful against my lips and I felt my entire body go weak. Wow!

The doors of the truck opened. The weight on my back lifted.

"Dammit! When I find Pasha, I will kill him!" Sergei paced beside the truck.

I broke from the kiss and put a finger on Pasha's lips for him to be quiet. I needed to be strong. I needed to be ready in case they spotted us. I needed to make sure my body wasn't completely melted, useless from Pasha's kiss.

He stroked my hair as I listened to Sergei and Danny.

"We have to get out of here, now!" Danny's voice wavered.

"And carry these fifty-kilogram bags back to the restaurant ourselves?"

"Leave them! The police will be here soon."

"I think he's hiding," Sergei said. "Pasha's around here somewhere. I bet he got wind of our job and he's hiding."

Shit. I checked my watch. I whispered to Pasha, "Three minutes more and the police will be here."

Sergei shouted a command at Danny. "Go look over there."

Danny ran off, probably toward the bushes, Sergei continued to pace.

Pasha squeezed his arms between the truck and me, effectively putting his arms around me. "A lot can happen in three minutes."

My nipples hardened. I could feel him grow even

bigger against me.

The possibilities of what Pasha and I could do got me excited until I heard Sergei say, "What if he's under the truck?"

I got ready to kick. Wait a minute. What was I thinking? If I kicked his face in when he looked underneath, I might kick too hard and have to explain my superior strength to the police. There were a ton of risks. I might kick too hard. I might be called into the police for questioning. I might get Pasha in trouble. Just way too many outcomes. None of them appealing.

I picked up a stone from the ground and threw it across the road several yards away into some bushes, opposite Danny's position. The stone rustled the leaves.

"Now I got you." Sergei ran off to follow the sound.

Pasha kissed me, his arms holding me tight in an embrace that never felt so strong, so good. For an odd moment, I felt as though he were taking care of me and not the other way around.

His lips held the hint of mint. He smelled earthy, like oak trees. I wanted to spend the entire evening kissing him under this crazy truck. My legs wanted to wrap around him and rub at a growing itch.

Danny and Sergei ran back to the truck.

"Did you find him?" Danny managed to say, puffing to catch his breath.

"If I found him, would I be standing here alone?" Sergei barked.

"Okay," Danny said. "Did you check under the truck?"

Shit.

Pasha held me tighter. "I got you."

I choked at his bravery.

"Chyort voz'mi!" Sergei cursed, stamping his foot.

"What?" Danny said.

"Listen," Sergei bit out.

I heard it, too. The high-pitched wail of police sirens.

"Let's get out of here," Danny insisted.

"Not without the package. Sukhorukov will kill us if we don't have it," Sergei said. The weight of the truck lifted. They must have grabbed the goods from the back of the truck and ran off, but sounds of other police cars came from the direction the guys were headed.

I whispered, "Hang on a sec." I poked my head out from under the truck and in the distance saw the police cuffing Sergei and Danny. A man spoke and gestured wildly at the police. He was probably the store owner explaining what had happened.

Pasha also poked his head out to see his "friends" getting arrested. "Sergei and Danny worked for Sukhorukov?" He tsked and shook his head.

"Who's Sukhorukov?"

Pasha scowled. "He is mafia boss. I did not know

he worked in St. Petersburg." Pasha glanced around. "Is safe to leave, now."

"Good idea. Before Sergei or Danny point out the truck," I said.

Pasha crawled out and stood. He offered his hand to me and helped me up. We snuck into the truck and drove off into the night.

The mafia boss. Sukhorukov. The name of the man who had my father killed.

# CHAPTER 17

I SPENT the next four days trying to come up with a strategy on how to locate Sukhorukov, infiltrate his restaurant, and stop him from committing more crimes.

Locating Sukhorukov was not the real problem. He likely camped out at Tkemali restaurant. Infiltrating the restaurant was also not a challenge. I could wiggle my hips into getting at least a part-time position there, I was sure of it. No, the real problem was how to stop him. What would it take to make sure he'd never hurt anyone again?

I remember one night my mother had came home from her government assignment covered in blood. After she washed up, she sat me down on the couch.

"I killed someone tonight."

I gasped. As far as I knew, she had never killed anyone before. Later I learned I was right. This had been her first and only kill.

She bore hard into my eyes. "Don't ever kill someone. There is never a good reason to kill. There's always a better way for people like us. We are strong. We can overcome anyone. For us, killing is wrong in every circumstance."

That night changed her. From then on, whenever the radio announced an arrest of a murderer, Mother would say, "Good. Lock him up and throw away the key."

Delivering Sukhorukov to justice was different. He never got his hands dirty, as far as I could tell. He never committed any of the crimes himself, just gave the orders. I couldn't exactly call in a personal favor like my mother sometimes did when she wanted the FBI to intervene or make an arrest. This was Russia. I had no connections here.

I opened up to my current surroundings.

The freezing night air felt good against my skin as I walked beside Pasha.

Earlier, during dinner, Vlad had told Pasha in Russian, "Take Ariel out for a walk tonight to see the river. Inna and I are having Tole and Misha over." He then winked at Pasha.

After dinner, I had snuck into Pasha's room to retrieve his letter to Alex Mizi, the drunk driver who killed his foster parents. I had put on my coat and we had set out for our stroll.

The Neva River was about a twenty-minute walk

away. Even bundled up, the air was freezing.

As we walked, I removed the envelope from my coat pocket. "I saw this letter by your bed. The one addressed to the man who killed your foster parents. Did you want to mail it?"

He made a face I couldn't decipher. "Oh. It's nothing. I maybe throw it away."

"You should mail it. Your words can change his life around, get him out of his living room."

Pasha didn't reply.

"I know." I put up my hands to concede. "Forgiveness is very hard, and carrying that weight can feel like a punishment itself. But if you do forgive him, he may not be the only one whose life will be changed."

Pasha stopped walking and looked at me with a blank expression. Uh, oh. Was he going to yell at me? Laugh at me?

"I'm sorry, Pasha. It was none of my business. I shouldn't have brought it up."

"Give me the letter."

I handed it to him. He took out the letter and looked it over. I peeked over his shoulder and read it again, translating the Russian in my head.

Dear Alex,

I am the foster son of Mr. and Mrs. Iltchenko. I want you to know that I do not hate you for what you have done. My parents considered you a good friend, so to honor them, I think of you with the same respect.

However, what you did was wrong and you must rectify your actions. You must live your life for three people now: my mother, my father, and yourself. You must contribute to the community for three people.

For yourself, become a member of Alcoholics Anonymous. You can help the community most by helping yourself.

For my mother, volunteer at Alcoholics Anonymous. Help others avoid making the same mistake you have made. Tell them your story.

For my father, volunteer to speak at schools, to teach students the dangers of drinking and driving. Again, tell your story. You can be the inspiration that saves people's lives.

Not only must you contribute to the community for three people, but you must also enjoy life for three people.

My father loved the zoo. Go on trips to the zoo and open yourself up to world of animals.

My mother loved museums. Visit the local museums and let the paintings and sculptures inspire you in ways you might have never imagined.

For yourself, do whatever you enjoy. Play your favorite sports, walk your favorite hikes, play music, draw, paint. Whatever you enjoy doing, act on the opportunity.

Living life for three people can feel like a huge responsibility, but to me it's the only way you can redeem yourself.

Sincerely,

Pasha

Pasha folded up the letter, stuffed it back in the envelope, and took a few steps to the street corner by the trash can. He licked the envelope closed and stuck the letter in the mailbox near the trash can. Alex Mizi would soon get Pasha's letter.

My chest warmed up with admiration.

"Let's go." Pasha forged ahead with a brisk step.

I jogged to catch up to him and took his hand. An abundance of compassion spilled from my heart.

WHEN WE REACHED the Neva River, I gazed across the river admiring the Peter and Paul Fortress, its spires lit up by spotlights. Taking Pasha's arm for warmth and comfort against the biting wind, I watched the river waves roil in the strong current.

We stood gazing at the rolling water for a good forty-five minutes not saying a word. We needed the time for Pasha's deed of mailing that letter to sink in. The stars winked at me as if to remind me of Vlad's wink at dinner, a secret the stars were keeping from me.

I held Pasha's arm tighter against the cold. "Who are Tole and Misha?"

"Friends. Inna first is friends with Misha, then Inna met Tole. Inna was, how is it you say, matchmaker, and they are now married."

"That's sweet."

He patted his pockets. "Oh, I left my phone at apartment! Can you get it?"

What? Why should I walk alone all the way back to the apartment just to get his phone?

I said, "We can go back together. Once we're there, you can quickly get your phone and then we can return here."

"No, I must wait for friend here."

"Which friend?"

"Uh…"

I took his arm. "You know what I like about you, Pasha? You're a terrible liar."

He gave a sheepish grin. So cute.

"Pasha, what is it you really want?"

"Go to apartment. Enter quietly and peek into living room from hallway. Maybe you find my, uh, phone."

I shrugged. "Okay. I'll be right back." Pasha was hiding something. I wondered if this scavenger hunt was all a ruse so that he could meet up with someone else. Another shady friend, perhaps? I hoped not. Curiosity got the better of me. I could rush to the apartment, check if any actual phone was there, rush back and see if Pasha met up with a distasteful character.

When I knew I was out of view from Pasha, I raced to the house making the twenty-minute walk turn to a twenty-second run. I could have arrived sooner, but the wind put up good resistance, slowing me down and chilling me to the bone.

Too eager to wait for the elevator, I jogged the four flights of stairs taking five stairs at a time. Opening the front door quietly was simple enough. The door didn't squeak or make any other compromising sounds. I closed the door behind me and poked my head from the hall to peer into the living room.

Jeepers creepers! Inna and the blond-haired man that must have been Tole were on the couch kissing. Inna had her hand inside the unzipped fly of Tole's pants. He had his hand tucked up her dress. By the way she was squirming on his hand, Tole knew what he was doing. The two of them glanced at the floor. For good reason. A woman with her brown hair up in a bun was on all fours, her skirt raised above her waist, her panties at her knees. She must have been Misha. Vlad crouched behind her pressing his face into her pussy.

Was this what Vlad's wink had been about? He had told Pasha to take me out for a walk and he winked at Pasha. If this swinging sex session was what Vlad referred to with his wink, that would mean

Pasha knew about their extra-curricular activities. They wouldn't let their own son know, would they? Adopted or not.

Misha's eyes widened as Vlad pushed his cock into her. I felt a tingling and wanted those eyes to be mine. I wanted the Wolverine to fill me with his manhood, his strength, his desire. By the wetness I felt between my thighs, I knew this passion of mine was not going to be fleeting anytime soon.

I licked my fingers and put my hand down my jeans to scratch the itch.

Inna put her head down onto Tole's lap. His head fell backwards, accepting the ecstasy Inna must have been giving him.

This changed everything. Inna might never be jealous of Vlad having sex with another woman. Did that open the doors for a possible tryst? Having a fling with Vlad could be the perfect relationship. An idea I tucked away for later.

Misha's belly was now flat against the carpet as she got hammered by Vlad. I imagined that was me he filled, my nipples rubbing against the carpet, my ass being spanked by his waist.

I rubbed myself to a higher dreamy state.

"You like?"

Shit! I yanked my hand out of my pants and spun around.

"Shh." Pasha put his finger to his lips. He took me down the hall toward my bedroom. "Your face looks nice when it is red."

His attitude clinched it. This wasn't the first he knew about his parents swinging with another couple.

I put my hands in my back pockets. "I guess we should get out of here."

"You want to go? We can stay if you like to watch."

I bit my lip and thought about the consequences. A tricky task to do when your nipples ache to be touched. And pinched. And sucked.

I craned to look around the corner back at Vlad and Inna in the living room. Across the room, Vlad and Misha stood, Misha pinned against the wall, her legs wrapped around Vlad. His muscled arms held her up and above his legs, his hot butt clenched with every thrust. Inna sat bouncing on Tole's lap, her dress obscuring the very thing that must have caused her to thrash about.

As I watched, I knew I didn't want to leave. But I wasn't about to let myself get turned on in front of Pasha. That would lead our friendship into a place of intimacy, a place I couldn't allow us to go.

Pasha's hands kneaded my shoulders. My stiffness and my body melted under his massaging touch.

I watched Vlad pounding in and out of that lucky woman. That could be me, I told myself. If Inna didn't mind Misha fucking him, then so could I.

My breathing lost its steady rhythm. My blood heated and raced out of control. I needed something between my legs. Something to be the Wolverine. A finger, a bottle, a baseball bat, something.

I placed my hand just above the waistline of my pants, wanting to dip my fingers inside but not in front of Pasha.

"I got you. Relax." Pasha ran his hand over mine and inched further down beneath the waistline of my panties.

I grabbed his wrist. "No, Pasha. I shouldn't."

"You don't want?"

I sighed. Vlad was thrusting faster now. My wetness dripped. "I do want it, but…"

"I do, too. Relax."

His fingers caressed my curls, then my clit. I moaned, giving in. Wasn't this wrong? I was getting turned on by thoughts of Vlad, not Pasha.

Wasn't this like cheating on Pasha? Maybe not cheating, but deceiving him?

Inna cried out a high-pitched squeal. Tole pushed his waist up to meet Inna's rapid bounces. I could tell by Tole's clenching face he reached climax. Inna's expression of bliss revealed how much she relished the release Tole sprayed inside of her.

Pasha put his free arm around my shoulders. From the corner of my eye, I noticed Pasha engaged with my every response to his titillating fingers that rubbed my clit in circles, spinning me dizzy.

He whispered, "You are attracted to Vlad?"

Oh, geez. Was it that obvious? I didn't reply.

"Is okay." Pasha's fingers continued driving me to bliss. "He is handsome."

Vlad bolted into Misha, then held her still, his body shaking, his muscles completely flexed. He must have been coming inside of her, too. I put my fists against my nipples and pressed, hoping it was a little more subtle than outright squeezing my breasts in front of Pasha. He got the hint that I was reaching full arousal. He pushed a finger in just past the entrance. I clenched around it, sighing at the delicious sensation of having him inside me. Wishing he were Vlad.

His arm around my shoulder caressed me. "Beautiful. You are so beautiful."

Was this wrong? Was this right? I hated not knowing. I needed everything to be black and white. But I remembered what Pasha had said during the class test. Even if someone told me the answer, right or wrong, Berlioz or Brahms, it was my decision. I let this moment be right. I chose it to be right.

Inna took Misha's arm and pulled her to the floor. What was going to happen next? The men were spent.

As Misha lay on her back, Inna dipped her head between Misha's thighs, no doubt lavishing Misha with her tongue. *So Inna goes both ways.* It made me reflect on every time Inna touched my arm, caressed my hair. She wasn't just being nice. She wanted me.

Pasha wiggled his fingers inside me. My climax

was just around the corner. He supported me with his arm around my shoulders.

He whispered to me in Russian, "Relax. Let it happen, my beautiful one. I've got you. I'm here for you."

Sparks crackled through every nerve in my being. I lusted at the strong way Vlad stood, his feet planted on the ground, shoulders width apart, his hands on his hips, his glistening cock displaying the evidence of his recent gift of passion.

Tole walked on his knees to Vlad and, oh my God, took Vlad in his mouth. Tole passionately applied his tongue, licking clean his wife's pleasure from Vlad's length.

I had never seen two men go at it together. How did I feel about it? It was such a turn-on. Twice the muscles, twice the strength, twice the men.

My juices dripped all over Pasha's hand as he cupped me, nearly lifting me off the floor.

I wanted that. I wanted to worship the Wolverine on my knees. I wanted to show how I understood his loner lifestyle. I wanted him to favor my skills, put his hand through my hair, smile down upon me as if I were the best he's ever had.

Misha cried out. Inna had successfully cleaned her empty of Vlad's cum, and covered herself with Misha's juices. Inna's face positively sparkled wet with Misha's bliss.

I felt my own peak approaching and grabbed hold

of my breasts.

"Yes," Pasha said in Russian. "Let it happen. You are so beautiful at this moment. I'm here for you. I'm here."

Vlad picked Tole up and pressed his face and body against the wall. Tole's cheek mashed to the wall and he had a smile of ecstasy on his face as Vlad pushed a finger in his ass.

I moaned. This was it. I was going to climax on Pasha's hand. How did I even get here? How did I get to this place of watching two couples in full swing while writhing on Pasha's fingers?

I gasped and bit my lip to stifle the orgasm escaping through my heavy breath.

Pasha's arm held me tighter. "I've got you."

My pussy clenched around his fingers. My body trembled, shaking and convulsing. I put a hand over my mouth to keep from crying out my ecstasy.

Pasha didn't stop. He thrust in me with his strong fingers. I reached another wave. And another, losing all control of my muscles.

In time, I could breathe deep again. Pasha's arm around me soothed me. I welcomed the comfort. I was also glad Pasha held me up with a firm hand cupping me between my legs, for my weakened knees would have surely collapsed from beneath me. Pasha kissed my cheek. "Are you okay?"

I swallowed, closed my eyes and nodded.

Pasha gently released me to stand on my own two

feet. "Let's take a walk." He took my hand in his. We snuck out the front door.

WE HELD HANDS and walked back to the ocean. The biting cold night kept my purring body awake. It was wrong for me to hold his hand. It was like I was giving him the wrong idea of there ever being an "us." But I needed his hand. I wanted his comfort. Still, he needed to know.

"Pasha, just because I'm holding your hand, I don't want you to think it means anything. It's just that I..." How was I going to put it?

He said, "You do not have to be alone."

I let go of his hand. "Pasha, we can't..." I rolled my eyes. How could I explain? "We just can't, okay?"

He stood still, then nodded. "You need comfort." Pasha spoke to me in Russian. "You need someone right now to be here for you. Anyone. And I happen to be the nearest friend." He held out his hand.

I smiled and took his hand. He understood. That was a relief.

We walked in silence. It bothered me that I couldn't share my secret with Pasha. I may have broken his heart, but it was better than the truth breaking his neck. If he knew my secret, it would just put his life in jeopardy as it had my dad.

In the quiet of the night Pasha and I strolled under the stars, his warm palm against mine. I thought back to my senior year in high school, the time when keeping my mother's secret hurt most.

I had been sitting beside my best friend Darlene outside the auditorium on the redwood steps. Together we soaked in the sun, chatting about risqué necklines, stuck-up teachers, gnarly math problems, and cute guys. We set up plans to go over math homework together after school at my house. While Darlene described the dress she planned to wear at the prom, my crush Chris Whetherston ambled up to us. His gaze stayed fixed on me. He wore a half grin as if he knew a secret that would cause me to die of embarrassment if anyone found out.

"Ariel." His voice speaking my name sounded so sweet I could practically taste it. "Will you be my date for the prom?"

My face flushed hot. I froze wondering if I had heard him right. I felt certain that he could hear my pounding heart. This must be a dream, a dream coming true.

Darlene whacked my shoulder playfully. "Ariel, don't keep the man waiting. Yes, Chris. She will go to the prom with you." She giggled.

He glanced back and forth between Darlene and me, an unsettled smile on his lips.

"Yes," I managed to say.

"Good," he beamed. "I'll pick you up at eight."

I couldn't remember much of what happened next. I was in a daze for the rest of the school day. After school, I hiked home uphill alongside Darlene who couldn't stop exhibiting the excitement I felt about the upcoming prom.

Darlene laughed. "And when Chris asked you out you were all like, duh..." She grabbed my arm. "Oh! I forgot to tell you. I saw your mother pick up a car last night. I can't believe I forgot to mention it earlier."

"What?" My gut clenched.

"It was amazing! You know that alley behind Sylvester's Diner? Some car plowed through. The driver must have been drunk. And there was this homeless guy. And the homeless guy was hobbling down the alley. He must have been a war vet because he had on fatigues. Anyway, the car swerved to avoid hitting the homeless guy. Then the car crashed into the side of the alley and the driver was all, like, huddled over the steering wheel. He must have been out cold."

"A car crashed?"

"Yeah, I was on my way home from visiting Caroline. You know how she's been out of school these past few days? Because she's been sick? So, yeah, I was coming home from dropping off her homework, and I happened to pass by the alley just as the car crashed and I was like, oh my god! Then your mom was there on the sidewalk, way down on the opposite side of the alley. She must have heard the car crash. She was looking all around on her side of the street like she was trying to get help."

My mother trying to get help? Nuh uh. More like making sure no one was watching.

"How do you know it was my mother? I mean, it could have been someone else, right?"

"Ariel, I've seen your mother before. She was even wearing that heathered, coral gown with the spaghetti straps that you showed me last week. The one hanging in her closet? She looked like she was coming from a date. Did she have a date recently? Oh, Ariel, that would be so cool! You with Chris and your mother with a guy at the same time."

"Darlene!" I gestured my frustration. Especially frustrated that after my mother had attended the Governor's dinner the previous night, she hadn't mentioned anything about a car crash.

"Whatever. So the driver was just hanging there unconscious, his car door wedged against the alley wall, and your mother comes up—" Darlene bent over at the waist and curled her arms to show her words. "She grabs the bottom of the car on the passenger side and actually picks up the whole car and pulls it away from the alley wall. Then she, like, rips off the driver's crumpled door and helps the driver out of the car. She didn't tell you? She must have told you. I mean, it was amazing! I was going to call you about it but as soon as I got home, my mom gave me a lecture about coming home late and not calling and she tried calling me but I forgot I had my phone off and now dinner was cold and blah, blah, blah. So she was all upset and I didn't feel like talking to anyone. Look, when we get to your place we can ask your mom about it and she can tell—"

"Please don't." Tears spilled down my cheeks. "Please, Darlene. Don't say anything to anyone about this."

"Why?"

"Just don't. Please. Not Mother. Not anyone."

Darlene looked baffled.

"Please, Darlene?"

Darlene scowled, keeping quiet as if trying to understand what the big deal was. She then shrugged. "Okay."

Relieved, I dried my eyes and walked with her the rest of the way home. By the time we got there, we were both thirsty. I told Darlene to wait in the living room and I fetched us glasses of water. In the kitchen, I heard the sounds of Mother coming home through the front door and cheerfully meeting and greeting Darlene in the living room.

I sipped from my glass and returned to the living room with Darlene's glass.

My mother asked Darlene, "What do you mean you saw me lift a car?"

I dropped the glasses. They shattered and water

spilled on the floor. "Darlene, you promised you wouldn't tell!"

I ran upstairs to my room and jumped onto my bed. My crashing world poured from my eyes.

Not again. Not this time. Not now.

Another end to my friends. Another end to my routine. And now an end of my new love life with Chris.

Darlene's distant voice called from downstairs. "I'm sorry, Ariel."

I wanted to rip Darlene's throat out. She had no idea what she had done. None.

"I'll see you tomorrow," Darlene called out. "Okay?"

I didn't bother to reply. I heard the front door open and close. Likely the sound of Darlene leaving. I heard approaching footsteps. Mother entered my room.

"I have to ask you a Truth question," Mother said. A Truth question was one that I had to answer truthfully, one that if I lied could cost someone's life. "Can Darlene keep a secret?"

If I said yes, I could see Darlene the next day. I could see all my friends again. I could see Chris again and go with him to the prom.

And someone might be killed.

"No," I mumbled.

My mother nodded and her gaze fell to the floor. "I'm sorry, Ariel. We better start packing."

Another move to another town.

I had to start all over again. If my life was made up of making close friends just to lose them, what was the point of making friends at all?

Secrets destroyed relationships. As long as Mother had these secret powers, as long as I had to keep this secret, I could never be in a relationship.

We had moved early the next morning and I never saw Darlene or Chris again.

Pasha had been quiet while we walked down the street. I glanced at him. The silence between us had become uncomfortable.

I searched for something appropriate to discuss. "How long have you known about your parents and their lifestyle?"

He returned to practicing his English. "I discover this one year ago."

"Just last year?"

He nodded. "I always knew they are hiding something. I thought it was something about sex. But one year ago, I see them with Tole and Misha, and I see what is their secret."

"Do they know you know?" Even though I enjoyed holding Pasha's hand, the outside of my fingers were getting numb in the cold.

"When I walked in, they saw that I discover them."

"What happened?"

"Vlad, he try to explain, but I am not mad. I just

am laughing. I tell him it is okay and I leave to let them have their fun."

"That had to have been quite a shock, though." I let go of his hand and put my hand in my coat pocket. "My fingers are cold."

He put his arm around me. The warmth of his body against my side felt good.

I looked up at his chiseled face. "Have you ever done it?"

"What?"

"Been with multiple partners at once?"

"No."

"But you've dreamed about it?"

"No. It is not my thing. And you?"

I shrugged into his sideways embrace. "I've fantasized about it, but I could never actually go through with it." I tilted my head to rest on his shoulder. "I don't think it's exactly the safest way of having sex, either."

He clenched my body closer to his side. "We are the same, you and me."

I wanted to think about how Inna let Vlad have sex with Misha, and the possible doors that opened for a chance to get to feel Vlad inside me. I wanted to think about the steps I needed to take to seduce my way into a part-time job at Sukhorukov's restaurant. I wanted to think about the best way to stop Sokhurokov from committing more crimes. But for some reason all I could think about was Pasha, the way he always made himself there for me and listened to my every need.

I squeezed closer to his side, relishing the warmth he offered. The street lamps dotted our path like stars with secrets lighting our way into an uncertain future.

# CHAPTER 18

THE next morning, I rubbed my eyes against the sun. What would it be like to talk to Vlad and Inna now that I knew their secret? Would Inna be willing to share Vlad with me? I flipped the bed covers off me, bounced out of bed, slipped off my thermal underwear, and went to my bedroom window to greet the sun's warmth. My eyes closed, my lungs sucked in a deep breath, my naked skin baked in the radiance.

If Inna was comfortable with letting her husband have sex with other women, a tryst with Vlad seemed ideal. He wouldn't be looking for a commitment from me. He was already married. Any relationship we'd have would be temporary, because I had a plane ticket to return to the U.S. in ten months.

*By the time I start working for the government right after college graduation, any sexual connection I've had with Vlad will be insignificant to my enemies.*

It was one thing for my enemies to seek out and kill a loved one of mine. My past fuck buddies, however, would never be in jeopardy.

What to wear? If today was about to be anything remotely to what I hoped, the day called for putting on some sultry clothes and some sweet lingerie. I slid my favorite pink panties up my long legs. To make sure I'd have the opportunity to show them off, I put on an orange mini skirt. I topped it off by tugging an orange tank top over my breasts to match my mini, without bothering with a bra. In the mirror I noticed the tank top was not only form-fitting, but it was also a tad see-through. My nipples poked out and the pink of my areolae showed. I looked too slutty.

Gripping the base of my tank top, I yanked it off over my head. I didn't have a pink or orange bra to match my ensemble, so I went with a crimson lacy push-up bra. After putting the top back on I checked myself in the mirror.

I imagined what Vlad would think when he saw me, how he'd grab me in his arms. "Ariel, your beauty is taking control of me. I must taste your breasts. I must explore your beautiful legs." He would glide his hand up my thigh, hitching my skirt with his wrist. "I must discover where these soft legs of yours meet," he'd say.

I'd tingle at his touch. Hell, I was tingling already.

He'd slip his hand down my panties and dip his finger inside me. I'd moan.

Two of his fingers would wiggle in making me squirm. "It's somewhere inside here, that special spot, that point inside you where your passage ends. I just need to go deeper."

I squeezed my breasts at the fantasy, my nipples pebbling through the fabric.

Inna's voice called out, "Ariel, there is breakfast now if you like."

"I'll be right there." I adjusted my clothes and dashed out my bedroom, butterflies of anticipation to see the Wolverine whimper in response to my outfit.

INNA HAD ONLY two places set at the kitchen table. From a pot on the stove, she scooped buckwheat porridge into the bowls.

Vlad was nowhere to be seen. So much for getting a response for dressing up sexy. "Where's Vlad? And Pasha?"

Inna's eyes widened when she saw my outfit, looking pleased. That made me feel a little better. At least someone appreciated my fashion choices.

She set down a box of raisins and sugar on the table. "They are at university."

I sat at the table. "On a Saturday?"

"Pasha has books to return to bookstore. Vlad goes with him to visit university library."

I took a bite of the oatmeal. It tasted plain.

Inna shifted the box of raisins closer to me. "Here. It makes oatmeal more sweet."

I thanked her.

She adjusted the hem of her short dress. I admired the floral pattern.

It was strange knowing how much Inna liked women. I felt more conscientious about my body. Was I turning her on? Did she have fantasies of me? Did I feel comfortable with that? I noticed the rise of my breasts with my every breath, the air in the room against my bare legs.

"Is something wrong?" Inna frowned.

I must have been overthinking this whole interaction we were having. Still, I couldn't get the image of her between Misha's thighs out of my head. My legs got goosebumps at the thought.

I took in a deep breath to build up my courage. "I need to tell you something."

"Yes?"

"I saw you. Last night."

A light of understanding glowed in her eyes.

I needed to explain. "When I went out with Pasha, something happened, and I had to go back to get something. I saw from the hallway that Vlad was with Misha, and you were with Tole."

She smirked and tilted her head, as if expecting more.

I told her the rest. "I also saw Vlad with Tole. And you with Misha."

I had trouble meeting her gaze. Suddenly I didn't feel like eating.

"Why you are telling me?"

I didn't understand her question. "Excuse me?"

"I am only wondering. Why you don't keep it a secret?" she asked, curiosity in her voice.

I wasn't expecting that response. I thought she might get angry, embarrassed, or even defensive.

"It's just that I thought it would be best not to hide anything. I thought I should, you know, come clean."

"That is it?"

"What do you mean?"

She shrugged. "Now you know Vlad has sex with other women. He is a very handsome man."

My face burned. She had me pinned down, knew exactly what I wanted.

She took my hand in hers. "Do you like Vlad?"

Her fingers were warm against my skin. I nodded.

"Come with me." Holding my hand, she guided me to the living room. "The only rule Vlad and I have is that we share." She took me to the couch and sat me down.

My heart pounded. She was giving me permission to make love to Vlad, but on the condition that I also make love to her.

Sitting beside me, she stroked my arm. "You have been with a woman?"

"No."

"Close your eyes."

I did. There was nothing to notice but her delicate fingertips against my arms. Then I felt the softest lips kiss me. I stiffened and when she broke the kiss, I opened my eyes .

She caressed my face. "Shh. Is okay. Close your eyes."

Closing them again, I felt her kiss my cheek, once, twice. On my lips a lingering, gentle kiss. My muscles tightened. My stomach tickled in a wild dance.

She ended the kiss. "Shh." She stroked my hair.

I let myself relax into her sensual hands, my head lolling, swaying to her touch. A yearning rippled across my skin. Perhaps she sensed my stirring desire when she placed a hand on my breast.

Gracing me with another kiss, she sent me to heaven. I loved her kisses. My nipple pushed against my bra to meet her palm. Was I taking advantage of her? Using her to get to her husband? Or was she taking advantage of me, using her husband as a way to get her hands all over my body?

She slipped a teasing tongue across my lips and instantly my questions didn't matter anymore. Her fingertips drifted down my sides to the edges of my top. She gently lifted it up over my head. She smiled at me. I giggled to release the pent up nervous energy.

She placed a comforting hand against my cheek. "Shh."

She embraced me. I welcomed her warm hug and felt soothed by her. Her fingers quickly released the bra clasp behind me and she leaned away from me sliding my crimson bra off my arms. I wasn't expecting that. I felt exposed and crossed my arms over my breasts. She took my hands in hers. "Is okay."

Why did I feel uncomfortable? I felt perfectly fine when women who were strangers saw me naked. What was so embarrassing about having a woman I know see me?

She stroked my hair. "You are beautiful."

I felt strangely relieved by her words. Was that what it was? Did I fear my body would be a disappointment to her?

She lowered her head to my chest and took a nipple into her mouth. Her slick tongue delivered warm, wet tingles to my pebbling skin.

Did I ever think coming to Russia would be like this? Becoming intimate with my host parents? Both the father *and* the mother?

A realization of such dangerous liaisons sunk heavy in my gut.

"What about Pasha?"

The sound of her mouth coming off my nipple

clicked wet. My glistening bud felt cold in the air.

"Pasha doesn't need to know."

"But what if he finds out?"

"Shh." She caressed my face. "He will not." She kissed me. Even if a part of me didn't believe her, the rest of my entire body felt she was right. Everything felt right.

She kissed my other breast and a desire stirred within me to satisfy her. As her tongue traced loving circles around my pink nipple, I raised a hand and cupped her breast. She pressed her hand against mine. Through the cotton fabric of her square neck dress, I felt her bud harden. Her lips popped from my chest. She caught her breath, placing both my hands on her breasts. She closed her eyes and arched her back, guiding me to massage her full bosom in circles. I lost myself in watching her become aroused. Seeing her writhing body made my own breathing heavier. Why was I getting excited? Was I actually bisexual? No. It was something else. The power of it all. The power of making her desire me.

She stood up and peeled her black dress off of herself. "When I first met you, I tell myself, 'I want her.' "

She smiled. With one click of her hands behind her, her black bra snapped off her chest and her lovely breasts bounced free.

She sat back down and stroked my hair, shoulders, and chest. "Vlad, too. He tell me, 'When I first met Ariel, I want her.' "

"Really?"

"Yes. Really." She smiled and cupped my breast.

I shivered, excited that Vlad wanted me as much as I wanted him. My skin crackled alive under Inna's delicate touch.

She put her hands around my head and coaxed me closer to her chest. "Come. Kiss me here."

I hesitated. Was I really going to do this? The way my body tingled all over, the question seemed to be answered before it was ever asked.

I kissed her nipple, not entirely comfortable with the idea of putting my whole mouth over her breast. I placed tiny kisses around her nipple, showering her with adoration, honoring who she was, honoring her own beauty.

She ran her fingers through my hair and I could hear her breathing intensifying. That power came again and gave me a rush. If giving her these gentle kisses got her excited, what would more do to her?

I planted my mouth over as much of her breast as I could take in and inhaled, sucking her in. She moaned. I loved this. The strength I had over making her respond as much as I wished.

Troubled thoughts brewed inside my chest. Was this wrong? Was it wrong to make Inna my puppet? To make her dance and writhe at my command? No. She wanted this. She initiated it and asked me for it. But that wasn't what concerned me. I was enjoying this power trip. Controlling her gave me the pleasure I was feeling. Wasn't that wrong? And what about Pasha?

I had stopped kissing her breast and Inna looked at me with a question in her gaze. I remembered Pasha's lesson. What was right and what was wrong was my choice. Berlioz or Brahms.

"Brahms," I muttered and planted my lips on her breast, flicking my tongue over her nipple.

She gasped. My heart beat rapidly, causing raw fervor to course through my veins.

*Does this excite you, Inna? Does this make you go wild? What about this?*

I pushed my hand between her thighs and slipped it down the front of her lacy black panties, working my fingers across her folds. Too dry. I brought my hand out and was about to lick it wet. I decided against it and sat up.

Putting my hand to her mouth, I commanded, "Lick it."

She devoured my middle three fingers, making them moist with her tongue. My nostrils flared with arousal at the sight.

I removed my hand and shoved my wet fingers back inside her panties. Cupping her mound, two fingers wiggled inside her and she pressed herself against my hand. I rammed in and out of her wetness, smirking at the glorious pleasure of watching her squirm.

"Is this what you wanted?" I grabbed a bundle of hair behind her head. "Did you rub yourself thinking of me doing this to you?"

She could barely speak. She panted, "Yes."

The wet smacking sounds of my fingers inside her filled the room. I could smell her tangy arousal.

"Tell me your fantasy. What was it?"

She gasped almost breathless and clenched around my fingers. "I bring you to my bed. You lay down." A moan escaped her lips.

I watched her body twist, her chest rising and falling to my thrusts. My nipples swelled. "Then what?"

"I go between your legs." She grunted as my thumb circled her clit. "I drink you."

She was close, so I really let her have it. Careful not to overuse my strength, I thrust my fingers into her. She squealed a high-pitch wail. She was going to come.

I was dripping in my panties. "In your fantasy, how did I taste?"

She didn't answer. Her full body was rising off the coach.

I stopped my fingers and jostled her head. "How did I taste?"

"Sweet!"

I rewarded her with fingers vibrating in and out of her at superhuman speed. That set her over the edge. She grabbed my breast and cried out with the same high-pitched wail of hers I'd heard the night before. I slowed down my thrusts and became fascinated by the way her body shook. Her pussy throbbed around my fingers, signaling my power. I wanted more.

I stood and whisked off my panties from under my mini. "Time to see how accurate your fantasy was."

I climbed on top of the sofa and faced the wall with a foot planted on either side of her hips. Looking down at her face between my legs, I took her head. "Drink me." I buried her face into my pussy.

Her tongue cleaved into me, pushing against every wall of that most intimate part of me. Goosebumps bubbled across my skin.

*Is this everything you imagined it would be, Inna? Is this your dream come true?*

My body trembled. The questions didn't seem to matter. It felt like I was losing control and Inna was in charge.

I wasn't about to let the power fall into her hands. I pressed her face deeper into me, but it only made my problem worse. The deeper she wiggled that tongue inside of me, the less control I had.

And, oh, how I just didn't care anymore. A surge of warmth flushed through me. I curled my toes on the couch cushions and leaned my forehead against the wall.

Now she was flicking fast across my clit. Yes! That was the spot! I glanced behind me and saw her frantic hands servicing between her legs. I was glad she addressed her own needs as well as mine.

She continued to drink me, slurping in my every drop. But she'd have to open her throat wider. When my muscles clenched, I knew a flood was on its way.

I squeezed my breasts, finding that balance of contracting and relaxing my body closer to the brink.

She sucked and lapped my folds, and pushed a finger in deep. That did it. With one hand I forced her face along my entire cleft while my other hand pounded against the wall.

A scream I barely recognized as my own accompanied the music of my trembling body as I spasmed above her. She gagged struggling to drink in all of my pleasure. By her muffled high-pitched cry, I realized she was coming with me. My body slowly lowered down from the ethereal back to Earth.

I shivered, an aftershock of my climax.

Once.

Twice.

A sweeping calm took over. A buzz across my body remained.

When I climbed off the couch, I sat next to Inna and we held each other. "How did I taste?"

"It is better than I imagined."

We laughed. I held her closer, feeling her warmth comfort me.

Several minutes later, Inna kissed my cheek. She strapped on her bra, wiggled back into her form-fitting dress, and moved to the kitchen. A pang of guilt hit my heart when I thought of Pasha. But like Inna had said, as long as Pasha didn't find out about my indoor sports activities with Vlad and Inna, he wouldn't be hurt by it. Keeping such a secret was fine with me. Secrets interfere with relationships, so this secret would help extinguish any chance of developing intimacy with Pasha.

By the front door, Inna slipped on her red pea coat, clutched her matching shoulder bag, and opened the door. "I must do shopping. I left something for you on kitchen table."

"For me?"

She smiled and exited the apartment.

I stepped to the kitchen to see what Inna had left on the table. I laughed. It was a condom. How thoughtful.

# CHAPTER 19

I HUMMED a tune as I strutted around the kitchen in just my orange mini. Air fluttered up my skirt making me aware of how wet I still was down there. On the counter, I found the plastic wrap and tore a sheet.

"Ow!" I cut my thumb.

When applying my fingers to cut off a straight edge of plastic, the razor wire had cut into the pad of my thumb. The wound was minor. I sucked on it tasting the metallic flavor of blood on my tongue. Checking my thumb again, it looked okay. I wrapped the porridge. When I opened the fridge to put it away, the blast of cold air nipped at my chest.

I got fully dressed again, rolling nude stockings up my legs to keep my legs warm for when I went outside. Needing to check out some music books, I took the city streets to the University Library, hoping Vlad would still be there. My legs chilled. Out in the beautiful blue day, I passed several gruff men shouting out catcalls. I kept my azure blue handbag close to me, though I doubted there was any risk of horny men grabbing it. The way they ogled me, they were more likely to grab me than my bag.

While my pussy still purred from my session with Inna, I ached to have Vlad inside me. A safe, sexy man to have a tangle with. I trotted up the steps to the library, pulled open the glass doors, and entered.

The vast library made finding Vlad a challenge. If he'd already left, I was wasting my time. Before going to the music section, I wandered the narrow stacks of books. I found him in the photography section. My heart fluttered. He was slightly bent at the hips, his eyes trained on a row of books near the bottom of the shelf. Was he admiring the books that dealt with nude photography?

"Vlad," I whispered.

He turned to face me, then smiled, looking glad to see me.

I glanced left and right. No one was around. I stepped into his isolated aisle. I wanted him even more than before. Somehow the wicked idea of being taken in the library made my desire for him more urgent.

I gave him a hug. He seemed surprised. Keeping

my head close to his, I kept my voice low. "I know about your lifestyle. How Inna lets you sleep with other women."

His eyes widened. "Inna told you this?"

"I found out myself." I explained seeing Inna and him sharing themselves with Tole and Misha. He blushed. It was sweet. I clutched his arm. "I want you."

He didn't pull his arm away. "Now?"

"Right here."

He scowled. What was his hesitation? That we were in a public place? That he wasn't as attracted to me as I thought he was? No, that couldn't be it.

I quickly added, "I'm not looking for a commitment. I want you to stay with Inna."

"No. I understand. But it is Inna."

"What about her?"

"Inna and I, we share everything. Everyone."

Now I got it. "Inna already enjoyed me."

"She did?"

I nodded. "It's your turn now."

I dropped to my knees and unbuckled his pants. He gasped. The tiled floor was cold. He gasped when my hands unzipped his pants, trespassed inside his boxers, and confiscated his cock. His warm length twitched under my palm. The command I had over his arousal made me want to test how much power I actually had. I stole him into my mouth, his entire flaccid dick. With greedy lips, I added his ball sack.

My mouth was full. He placed his hands on the top of my head and exhaled. I didn't move. Not one naked inch. I just held his entire crotch between my lips and waited one beat.

He sighed and grew bigger.

Two beats.

He groaned and grew bigger.

Three beats.

He made a guttural sound and grew bigger.

By the expanding size of his length, I had to let his balls slip out from my mouth.

Four beats.

He pressed my head against his groin and grew bigger. I felt his tip tag the back of my throat.

Five beats.

He gyrated his hips, growing bigger, finding the only friction my mouth would offer him at my tonsils.

I gagged, then clamped down on his cock, swirling my tongue around him.

Desire coursed through me. I wanted this man. I wanted this Wolverine to plough me with his dick.

Letting him free from my lips, I stood, turned to face the stacks, and leaned against them, sticking out my butt. I looked over my shoulder at him to give him a seductive invitation. He flipped up my skirt and yanked down my leggings. I had to stop myself from squealing with glee.

He tugged down my panties as far as my knees. I felt his tip stroking along my entrance.

A shudder ran through me. "Wait. Let me get a condom. I don't want to get pregnant."

"You don't take pill?"

"No," I lied. I thought it more polite to have him think I was avoiding pregnancy than any STDs he may have.

I bunny dipped to the floor and opened my purse, taking out Inna's single foiled condom. I could practically taste his disappointment and couldn't blame him. The idea of having his bare cock inside made my arousal swim circles, but safe sex was my biggest rule. Especially with a man who shared himself with many women. My fingers ripped open the wrapper. I placed the rubber ring over his tip and rolled it down his length, stroking him in the process.

By the way he groaned, I may have just converted him to practicing safe sex more often.

I stood back up and assumed the position, bending over holding onto the stacks ready for whatever dish he served me back there.

He used his fingers and found my pussy once again, wet, waiting for him, needing him. Over the tops of the books on the shelf in front of me, I had a view of the rows of books on other shelves. I could even see some students browsing in the other aisles. No question they could see me, too, but they hadn't yet. One loud gasp or scream of ecstasy from these lips and our concealed activity would alert them. They'd get quite the view of me being hammered by my Wolverine.

My Wolverine pushed just his tip in. Was he teasing me? I wanted more and swiveled my hips to let him know.

He pushed in further, but not by much. "It is okay?"

Was he kidding? I was on my way to becoming the next Niagara Falls back there and he was wondering if he was hurting me?

"Deeper," I said.

He didn't get the hint, though. His rod didn't inch in, it didn't even centimeter in. What was he doing, testing the water? *Come on in, the water's fine!*

"Is okay?"

Oh, for crying out loud.

"Yes. Fuck me, already."

As late as it was, he finally got the memo and pushed all the way in. It felt incredible having his full length inside me. Then an idea popped in my head. I thought of all the other women Vlad had been inside – Inna, Misha, and other satisfied beautiful women. I thought of the way my pussy had been pressed against Inna's lips just moments ago and now was filled with Vlad's shaft. Inna sucked my pussy, now my pussy swallowed Vlad. As though I were the go-between for Inna to give Vlad a blowjob. A chuckle escaped my lips, then a gasp. Vlad had thrust himself in me so hard, it made the sound of our skin slap together.

"Why you laugh?"

Shit. "Sorry. It was unrelated."

"It is not good? What do you want?"

"Just give it to me hard. Don't be afraid." I didn't want to have to tell him that. I was expecting an alpha X-man, for Pete's sake. Instead I got a nice guy.

But if my laughter made Vlad angry, he turned his anger into giving me what I wanted. That sweet pumping he did brought me higher, jostling me into the bookcase. I was finally getting properly fucked by Vlad. In a library, no less. Did this make me feel closer to him? More intimate? It did. The secret we shared of being wicked in the library brought me feeling all sorts of layers of intimacy.

I felt him reach under my torso and find my clit. He rubbed it. I nearly collapsed right there. His thrusts made my body jerk against the stacks, causing the books near my hands to shift on the shelf.

Then Tanya appeared on the other side of the bookshelf. She was browsing the books on the other side of the shelf I was clinging to. My heart pounded at the excitement of being caught. Her eyes faced my direction scanning the books in front of her, and for a moment I thought she would pass without noticing us. I placed a hand over my own mouth just to keep from letting a sound out.

No good. Vlad shoved into me with delicious, brutal force and I gasped. Tanya noticed, her eyes shifted directly to me. She kept her focus locked on me as I jiggled from Vlad's firm pounding. He was oblivious to our audience. Suddenly my feelings of intimacy shifted from Vlad to Tanya. She put her hand under her shirt and touched her breast. She and I were sharing this moment of me getting fucked. And it became a secret. Our secret. I felt an intimate connection with her, even though Vlad was the one ramming his cock inside me.

Was this right? Was it right to hide this secret from Vlad? Hell, I was getting fucked by a married man in the University Library and I was worried about the morality of being caught by some woman who sleeps with her teacher? I was putting too much thought on it and decided to go with the flow.

I closed my eyes. Vlad was inside of me. Thank goodness he wasn't asking me if it was okay. His thrusts felt good, but they felt mechanical. He was inside me stretching me six ways to serenity, but was he with me?

I opened my eyes. Tanya was with me. Completely. One hand was down her jeans, now. That bulge of fingers swimming at her crotch signaled her passion. Like sign language, I could read how high her arousal was by the speed of her spelling. Though she had a hand up her shirt, her buxom chest couldn't hide her increased breathing.

If people could feel colors, I was feeling all shades of yellows and reds sparkling through my arms and legs. My heart pounded faster to drum along with the colorful festivity. Why was my body reacting to Tanya this way? I wasn't a lesbian. I wasn't even bisexual. It had to have been Vlad's cock plunging inside me, right?

But I knew the truth. Sure, Vlad felt great, but if I were using my fingers instead of his rod, I'd feel the same rainbow flood through my body. It was Tanya who brought me higher, not Vlad. It was from watching her get excited, and knowing it was me that got her excited. I remembered the power I felt over Inna, inducing her to moan and fill the room with her high-pitched squeals of pleasure. That same thrill came over me as I watched Tanya's chest rise and fall, her body writhing on her hand.

Those colors inside me burned brightly, flashing heat across my breasts, neck, and cheeks. I let my shoulders lean on the bookcase and gave my breasts the squeezing attention they ached for. My chest clenched, pushing out a drawn out, quiet whimper of my inevitable release. Tanya inched closer to my face, her eyes locked with mine above a cityscape silhouette of books. After making a contorted face, she let out a deep breath and shuddered a beautiful, silent climax.

*From me,* I told myself. *I controlled her. She came because of me.*

I gasped, tightened around Vlad's length, and shook. Tanya slipped her hand over the books to my face and held out her finger. I knew what she wanted. I wanted it, too. I wanted to taste the power I had over her. As the colors of my climax shot throughout my body, I let her finger enter my lips and tasted my power. Her tart wetness made my head spin. I hummed around her finger and heard Vlad growl his release.

Then he was still. I could almost hear the silence of the library fill the aisles.

Tanya took back her finger. Vlad softened inside me. I closed my eyes and puffed out any final traces of tension into a completely relaxed state. When I opened my eyes again, Tanya was gone. I still hadn't had sex with the Wolverine like the way I'd imagined, but at least it was amazing sex, thanks to Tanya.

Vlad pulled out from me. As he removed the condom and lifted his pants back over his hips, I tugged my panties back up under my skirt.

A thought occurred to me. All my life, secrets played a role in destroying my friendships and any chance of getting a boyfriend. Yet I had just experienced an amazing intimate moment with Tanya because of a secret. A shared secret.

"We go home now." He buckled his belt.

"Could you not tell Pasha about this?" I pulled up my leggings.

"Yes. I will not tell Pasha." He zipped his fly. "Let's go."

We walked back to his place in silence.

\*\*\*

DINNER WAS EXCRUCIATING. I wanted to hit someone, but knew that if anyone deserved a good smacking it was myself.

At first, sitting at the table was fine. Pasha was late so it was just the three of us, Inna, Vlad, and myself. Inna caressed my cheek as she served dinner, and Vlad held my hand, running his thumb over my fingers. I felt such incredible love from them, even though I knew it was a love for our new sexual relationship.

For the first time in a long time, I felt like this was a relationship that would work. Strong enough to feel the emotional connection I longed for, but short enough to know it was temporary, and I wouldn't be putting them in any jeopardy. I sat with Inna and Vlad, both lovers of mine, and we ate. Everything tasted a little better than usual. Even the soggy potatoes.

Inna cut a piece of beef with a smirk. "Vlad says you made good progress in the library."

My face burned hot. "Yes. He helped me get first-hand experience of St. Petersburg."

Vlad shrugged. "I did fill her in with my important details." His lips curled into a smile. "Inna says she tasted you." He held up a fork with a piece of beef and asked Inna, "Does she taste as good as your meat?"

"Better."

Vlad nodded. "I must try sometime." He reached for a drink of his glass of vodka.

Though my ears itched like crazy from the embarrassment I had over him speaking so brazenly to his wife about me, I wasn't about to let his suggestion go unchallenged. "Maybe tonight. For dessert."

Vlad sputtered from his glass. Both Inna and I laughed.

The sound of the front door opening and shutting filled the house. "Sorry I am late." Pasha trudged down the hall to his room, his voice loud enough for all of us to hear. "I had talk with my history professor." He joined us at the kitchen table. Inna served him a plate of beef, potatoes, and greens. "Looks delicious, Inna."

I stared down at my fork. A few quick glances at both Inna and Vlad revealed that they also kept their gaze to their plates.

Vlad broke the tension. "Pasha. Your school day? It was good?"

"Yes." He had an endearing boyish energy as he spoke through a bite of beef. "I learn simple way to write a fugue. It is so cool. Ariel, listen to this. First, write a short chord progression, two or four chords, then repeat it through whole piece. If motive is eight measures, it is played anytime chord progression repeats. You see?"

I didn't quite understand, but I nodded anyhow,

feeling the confusion Vlad must have felt when I explained how I picked up the refrigerator. The difference was I had the added bonus of feeling guilt.

Pasha waved his hand to dismiss me. "You no understand me. That is okay. I show you after dinner."

I jumped in and gave a hard stare at Inna. "Speaking of after dinner. There won't be any dessert tonight, right Inna?"

"Oh. Yes. There is no dessert."

Pasha scowled. "We never have dessert. Why do you say that?" He laughed, then remembered something. "Ariel, I almost forget. Tanya said to tell you she says hi."

My eyes widened.

Pasha took another bite of the beef. "You are being friends with Tanya?"

"Oh. Yeah. She may help me study for exams." The lie calcified in my gut forming a heavy stone.

"Is good. She is smart woman."

The rest of the meal consisted of Pasha explaining how to write a fugue. Though I finally understood the method he described, I couldn't take in his enthusiasm. My heart was already filled with stones of lies. There was no room to take in anything else.

# CHAPTER 20

T HE next morning from my bedroom doorway, I told Pasha to go ahead to school without me, that I would go on my own. Though he offered to wait, I convinced him not to and breathed a sigh of relief when he left. Still in my thermal underwear, I climbed back into bed. Why was I feeling such guilt over having sex with his parents? I never made a commitment with Pasha. I made it abundantly clear that I had no intention of being his girlfriend. Inna and Vlad weren't even his real parents!

So why did I feel such guilt?

There was a knock at my bedroom door.

"Come in."

Inna and Vlad entered. Inna sat at my side on the bed as Vlad remained standing.

Inna stroked my face. "How are you?"

"Fine." I emphasized the lie with as genuine a

smile as I could force.

Vlad stepped a bit closer. "You want to stop the sex, it is okay. You want to have continuation of the sex, it is okay, too."

Inna shifted her hips on the bed. "It is your choice. Okay?"

I put a hand on my chest and let out a sigh of relief. By ending our sexual escapades, I could put the tryst behind me as a past mistake. I could return to maintaining my friendship with Pasha. "Thank you."

Vlad turned to Inna. "We go now."

Inna explained. "Vlad is going to work. I am going to market. You go to school, yes?"

"Yes." I could feel the heaviness of my lies to Pasha crumbling away.

"Good." Inna kissed my forehead. They left my room closing the door behind them.

I GOT OUT OF BED once I knew I was alone in the house. After a quick shower, I heard a banging on the front door. Someone probably forgot their keys. Pasha was likely already on campus, so it was either Vlad or Inna. With my body still wet from being cleansed of yesterday's mistakes, I wrapped a towel around my torso, tucked it at the top of my breasts, and held it there as I strode to the door.

I opened it wide. A fist hammered into my face. A punch of pain burst across my nose and blinded me. I felt a hand place a damp smelly cloth over my mouth.

Dammit! The cloth was soaked in ether. Someone was trying to knock me unconscious.

I bit on his hand. He screamed. Still blinded by the pain pounding me, I waved my arms to feel where he was. Finding his collar, I lifted him off his feet and threw him out into the fourth floor hallway.

My vision, though blurry, returned. A man I didn't recognize lay in the hallway near the elevators. He looked startled by my strength. Slamming the door shut, I made sure he couldn't get into the apartment. As I felt myself losing consciousness, I realized locking the door was a futile attempt to stop him. If determined enough, he could always break down the door. I stumbled to my room.

I had to stay awake. I had to.

Finding my cell phone, I flipped it open.

I had to stay awake.

My fingers struggled to find Pasha's number.

I had to stay awake.

My eyelids became too heavy for me. It was time to call someone. Anyone.

Stay awake. I had to. I had to.

Darkness.

## CHAPTER 21

I FELT upside down. Blood filled my head, and my arms hung down. My nose throbbed with a nagging pain, but it was tolerable. Where was I?

I opened my eyes. The kitchen refrigerator appeared upside down from my vantage point. I must have been lying naked on the kitchen table with my head dangling off the end. Trying to raise my arms was a mistake. I felt wires cut into my wrists.

"Ah! You're awake." A deep voice said in Russian.

I raised my head to see who it was. The man standing beside the table was the same man who hit me at the front door.

I cleared my throat and spoke in Russian. "Who are you?"

"I like to think of myself as the fixer." He spoke

softly and moved about the kitchen the way a masseuse might prepare to give a massage. "When my employer Mr. Sukhorukov has a problem, I fix it. In this case, when your boyfriend Pasha didn't do the job he was hired to do, my employer decided he needed to be punished and called me to have me do whatever I desired to his girlfriend."

He'd stripped me naked. I could guess what he wanted to do to me. "Pasha's not my boyfriend."

"Is that so? These pictures seem to tell a different story." He held up his phone to my face and scrolled through photos of me holding hands with Pasha by the Neva River and resting my head on his shoulder. The pictures told me a truth I was denying all this time, that I did have strong feelings for Pasha.

He poured a bottle of vodka in a bowl and added a container of hot pepper. "Don't worry. I am not interested in raping you. I am only interested in pleasing you."

"So that Pasha can find me tied to the table, taken before he's had the chance to take me himself?"

"Something like that."

"Pasha won't care. Like I said, he's not my boyfriend." I shifted on the table and felt wire cutting into my ankles. If it had been regular rope, I could have easily ripped myself free. But this wire cut into my skin. Any attempt I made to rip free would end up ripping open my veins and arteries. "If you want to please me so much, why do the wires feel like razors?"

"Yes, I apologize for that. I didn't bring any silk ropes so I had to improvise. The best things I could find in this kitchen were the metal razor strips I peeled off from the plastic wrap and aluminum foil boxes."

Terrific.

He had a stack of hand cloths beside him. He picked one up and dipped it in the bowl of vodka. "Just relax, and enjoy this sensual experience. As I said, my only goal is to please you. The sooner you climax, the sooner I will leave."

I watched helplessly as he placed the wet cloth on my breast. At first the towel was cold, but that quickly changed to a tingling my nipple couldn't ignore. He soon added another cloth to my other breast. My nipples felt like hot tongues incessantly pressing and swirling against every inch. Not a burning, but a buzzing. He placed cloth after damp cloth of his concoction across my belly, hips, and thighs. I let my head drop back and enjoyed the crackling sparks of spice he incited on every crevice and peak of my body. Wetness dripped between my legs.

He squeezed the excess of another cloth into the bowl. "Perhaps you would like to taste the fire your body feels."

He placed the small cloth to my lips. It was alcoholic, but I welcomed it. The combination of the intoxicating drink with the spices sparked a fire I swallowed down. I sizzled on the inside as well as outside. He gently pushed more of the cloth in my mouth. I sucked in the delicious burn. Soon the entire cloth was inside my mouth, and if his goal was to put a gag on me, I enjoyed it.

The fixer dipped another cloth in the bowl. "When I was young, I had a girlfriend. She looked very much like you. I loved her with all my heart. I wrote sonnets and other poems for her."

As I sucked on the fire, I felt his hand massage me between my legs. The surface tingling on my body penetrated my skin and ran its course within me.

"Then one night, we were both feeling quite amorous. We agreed to make this night be our first time. She was just as beautiful naked as she was clothed. More than Venus. More than the Mona Lisa. No sculpture or artwork could ever capture her beauty."

His fingers opened me to a dildo of some sort. I couldn't see it. I didn't care to see it. All I wanted to do was experience it. As he pushed it inside, his fingertips ran back and forth across my clit like strings performing a tremolo. The heat overwhelmed me. The spicy fire pinched my nipples, burned across my belly, scorched my lips, and kindled my pussy.

"But it was my turn to undress. I was not gifted with a large—" He lightly pinched my clit. "She laughed at my size. She tried to stop me from leaving, and even apologized repeatedly. But my pride was too broken to be repaired. I eventually made it my life work to find how I can please women without sex. You are bearing the fruits of my lifelong study."

He worked the dildo faster inside me. I bit on the cloth and screamed a muffled cry as my orgasm raced through me. He gently pet my folds as I came down from the smoky clouds.

He removed the dildo. "I told you the truth. I'm going to leave you now that you had your climax. I will leave you to be discovered by your boyfriend. But there's one thing I left out. A simple fact about vodka…" He held up the dildo. It was a candle. "…is that vodka is flammable." He lit the candle.

My heart raced in fear.

He placed the candle back inside me. "This candle should last about ten minutes. Plenty of time to gather my things before you and the rest of the apartment goes down in flames."

I spat the cloth out of my mouth. "You bastard! Let me go!"

"Don't worry. After your boyfriend finds you, he won't grieve long. My next assignment is to punish him directly. To set an example to anyone else who crosses Mr. Sukhorukov."

Through the rag, I screamed at him to release me, but he ignored me. My throat scratched from my screaming and the spice. I couldn't see through the tears. I felt pathetic as my cries turned into begging and pleading. Even when I heard him leave out the front door, when no one was left to hear me, I still pleaded in pitiful whimpers to be released.

HOW MUCH TIME did I have left? Three minutes? Two minutes? I needed to escape. My head and arms dangled off the edge of the table and my arms were behind my head, my wrists tied with razor wire to the table legs. One option was to pull against the razor wire. It would slice my wrist to the bone and I'd need a tourniquet to stop the bleeding, but at least I'd be alive.

Probably one minute left.

*If I do pull against the wire, it would be better to yank at it, and not pull slowly. That would improve my chances of actually breaking the wire with less damage to my wrists.*

*I hope.*

There was no time to debate this. How much time did I have? Seconds? I made a fist and got ready to pull against one of the wires. Then I realized there was a better way. I could escape without removing the wires from my wrists.

I grabbed the table leg fastened to my wrist and ripped it off the table. The table wobbled on its remaining three legs, threatening to tilt. With the table leg still attached to my wrist, I reached, removed the lit candle in me, and blew it out.

With my teeth, I carefully unwound the wire from my wrist. The broken table leg dropped to the floor. I freed my other arm, sat up, and brushed off the damp clothes, like spiders on my body.

I hugged myself, shaking from being so close to death.

*Get a hold of yourself. It's over. Just work out what to do next.*

Pasha! I had to call Pasha and warn him.

I freed my ankles from the wires, limped to my room and found my phone. I called him. It went to voice mail.

Without leaving a message I hung up. What time was it? After three. He'd be finishing up his last class in less than ten minutes and had his phone off. From what the fixer said, they wouldn't kill him until after he went home and discovered my dead body. If that were true, I had to make sure he didn't go home after class. I dressed my wounds as quickly as I could and slipped into jeans and a T-shirt.

I called Pasha again. As I waited for him to pick up, I eyed my wrists. They were bandaged like I had just tried to commit suicide.

"Da?"

"Pasha, it's Ariel. You have to leave the city. Don't come home."

"You are saying what now?"

"You have to believe me. Mr. Sukhorukov hired someone to kill you as soon as you come home. You must not come home. Leave the city. Leave and don't come back."

"I do not fear death."

Damn him! I glanced at my bandages and pictured him someday slitting his own wrists. I had to shake him up, make him hate to see me.

"I had sex with Vlad."

"What?"

"And Inna. I had sex with both of them." My gut turned to stone. I felt like the worst person alive.

"When?" Pasha's voice choked.

"Yesterday. Before dinner."

Silence.

Pasha would never forgive me, but it didn't matter. He didn't know about my super abilities and how keeping such a secret meant never allowing myself the luxury of having a boyfriend. Saving his life was more important than maintaining our temporary friendship.

"Pasha?"

"Vlad and Inna are better off without me. I come home now. We talk." He hung up before I had the chance to reply.

It seemed nothing I said would change his mind. I needed to stop Mr. Sukhorukov. Now.

# CHAPTER 22

I LEFT the apartment, walked the few blocks to the subway station, and took the subway to Vladimirskaya station. I stormed up the subway steps five at a time, not caring who saw me.

This man thought he could kill my father, kill me, and kill Pasha just to set an example? This ended now.

Sukhorukov's restaurant, Tkemali, was inside Renaissance Hall, a modern hotel of glass across from the Vladimirskaya church. I stepped inside the hotel. Eight-foot tall Greco-Roman-type statues lined the walls. Signs pointed the way to the restaurant two flights up. I found the entrance. The doors opened up to a plush waiting room that doubled as a bar for early guests to nurse a drink while waiting for their table.

At the podium, a man in a navy blue suit asked in Russian, "Can I help you?"

His broad shoulders and bulging biceps looked like they were about to burst out of his tailored suit.

I circled around the podium and grabbed his throat. Picking him up by his neck, I pressed him against the wall, and replied in Russian. "Yeah. Where's Sukhorukov?"

His eyes widened with shock, revealing he'd never been pinned in such a compromising position in a fight before, much less by a woman. His meaty fingers struggled to peel off my hand choking his throat, with no effect.

"What's the matter? Too busy trying to breathe? Here. I'll give you something to keep your mind off that." I clamped my other hand around his balls and slowly squeezed.

He squealed, but said nothing.

"Where is he?" I asked.

He glanced to the back of the restaurant. Good. Sukhorukov was here. I changed my grip at his neck to go from cutting off his esophagus to squeezing the arteries on either side of his neck. That effectively stopped the blood to his brain. He dropped to the floor unconscious.

The patrons at the restaurant, as few as there were at this afternoon hour, avoided eye contact with me as I pushed past tables and chairs, knocking a few pieces of the furniture over in the process.

The swinging doors in the back were clearly marked in Russian, "in" and "out." Through the circular window, I saw a waiter coming toward me through the "out" door. I slammed the door into him causing his tray of hot soups to slap his face.

Another man in chef's whites shouted in Russian, "You can't be here!"

I grabbed a paring knife from the counter and flung it across the kitchen into his shoulder. He screamed and crumbled to the floor, but his cry was more likely from shock than from pain. Time to show him what screaming in pain felt like.

I crouched over him and twisted the knife in his shoulder. Blood seeped onto my hand.

"Where's Sukhorukov?" I demanded above his shouts.

He cried out in Russian. "Upstairs! Upstairs! He's upstairs!"

I wiped my bloody hand on my jeans and left the chef alone to work himself out. The stairs were in the back of the kitchen. At the top of the stairs down the end of a hall two guards stood, arms folded, in front of a door. One raised a handgun at me. As he began pulling the trigger, I ran with super speed to him and pointed the gun at his neighbor. Friendly fire got rid of one. The dead neighbor slumped to the floor.

I twisted the gun out of the shooter's hand. In Russian, I told him, "Give me a reason."

He raced down the hall and practically tripped downstairs.

I opened the door. A marble desk, a gold phone, a

bear fur rug. I wondered how many died just for Sukhorukov to feel so rich.

A fat man sat at the desk. He was in the middle of a conversation on the phone.

I said in Russian, "Are you Sukhorukov?"

He spoke into the receiver, "I'll have to call you back." He hung up the phone and replied in Russian, "I am Sukhorukov. Who are you?"

I sauntered over to his desk, sneered at the room filled with expensive, useless extravagance. "I'm the girl you tried to have killed today." I ripped the phone cord from the wall and flung the phone across the room. It smashed into pieces.

He smiled. "Are you trying to scare me?"

"No." I leaned over, clasping both ends of the tabletop. He leered down my shirt. "If I wanted to scare you, I'd do this."

I picked up the entire marble desk and threw that across the room, too.

*There* was the fear I hoped to see. "I guess you were right. I did want to scare you after all."

I stepped behind his chair.

Looking over his shoulder, he followed me with his gaze.

"But you see, it isn't just that you tried to kill me that makes me so angry. You also had plans to kill my boyfriend, Pasha." I only meant to call Pasha my boyfriend to help him know who I was talking about. Instead, the words sent an unexpected shiver down my body of something I so desperately wanted. Someone I could never have.

Sukhorukov jumped from his seat and ran for the door. With my super speed, I beat him to it. I stood in front of the door blocking his path. My gut turned toward painful memories.

"I wasn't the first in my family you ordered to be killed." I stepped closer to him. "You also killed my father, Cyril Garrison." I put an arm around his shoulder and whispered in his ear. "Now what would you do if you were in my position?" My whisper was filled with choked words. "Would you set an example? Would you light the killer on fire? Would you brand him with some stupid symbol?"

He huffed for breath. A bead of sweat dripped down his forehead. He said nothing.

"What would you do if you were me?"

He shivered in my grip and didn't respond.

"Would you do the right thing?"

"Y-yes. The right thing," he stuttered.

"And what would that be, hmm?" But I already knew the answer. What was wrong and what was right was my choice. "Berlioz or Brahms?"

He gulped. "What?"

"I choose Brahms." I yanked his chin and snapped his neck.

# CHAPTER 23

I DIDN'T even remember the walk to the smoky bar. Today was the first day I killed someone.

Letting that fact sink in felt like I was drowning myself. It made me wonder just how better off the world was with me in it. Gradually, the question changed and I wondered how better off the world would be without me.

"Buy you a drink?" The words were Russian, spoken by a young man with a head of hair that looked like a cute shaggy dog. Considering how close we were to the campus, I guessed him to be a college student.

I replied in Russian. "You, my good man, can buy me as many drinks as you like."

I tried different fruity drinks. Strawberry with vodka, pineapple with vodka, minty something or other with vodka, and who knows what else? After five drinks, I found out the story of the guy buying me drinks. He was an archeology major and had dreams of traveling across the Middle East to find undiscovered cities buried beneath the sand. In those same five drinks, I told him my story: I was wet and toyed with the idea of having his cock inside me. He liked my story very much.

Apparently, our conversation was fascinating because we quickly had seven other cute guys hover nearby to listen in. They were also nice men because they all bought me drinks.

I felt a strong bond with the guy with the shaggy hair. I felt like he understood me. Knew everything I was going through. And that was just what I needed. Shaggy's name was Derek. Or Daniel. Or something.

I held up a finger to emphasize a lesson I learned today. "He was wrong, you know."

"Who was wrong?"

"Pasha. He said. Get this, now. He said, 'What is right and what is wrong? That is your choice.' " I shook my head. "It's not my choice. It's not."

"I get you more drink?"

"Why are you talking funny? You know what I think? I think you need to work on your Russian."

"It is English. You speak English, so I speak English."

That didn't make sense. "I'm speaking English?" I practically busted up laughing. "I thought I was speaking Russian."

"You want more drink?"

I squinted at him and wagged my finger. "I know what you're trying to do. You're trying to get me drunk." I gasped. "Maybe you want me to pass out so you can have your way with me."

"No, no. Is just to help relax." He left and came back with another drink. This one was orange.

I raised my cup. "Salud!" Downed the entire thing and let the orange liquid burn away the guilt of having killed someone. "Let's see. I had green, red, yellow, pink, brown – horrible, that brown stuff. Don't give me any more of that. – pink, orange, and some other colors I don't remember. What's next?" Then I had the best idea ever. "I know! How about a white Russian?"

I leaned over and gave Daniel or Derek a passionate kiss. He put his hand on my breast and squeezed. All the other boys cheered.

Before any fun, I wanted to completely rid of that rock of pain in my gut. I waved the empty glass above my head. "If everyone else joins us with a few drinks, I'll show you all a good time."

The way they all clamored to the bar, I never saw so many boys eager to get their hands on a drink.

We all drank together, their joy mixed with mine. The more we drank, the louder we got. After a few more hours, the quieter we got. One by one, the boys were slumped in their chairs drooling. Derek or Daniel or Davy also had to nap. He had his head on the table. By the time I felt complete joy and wanted to take on the world, I was surrounded by sleeping lightweights.

"Losers." I lifted one boy's wrist to check the time. Just after seven in the evening. That cool heavy metal band Pasha showed me was playing soon. I let go of the boy's wrist and let it plop back onto the table by his sleeping head. "I'm gonna go out and find me a real man."

# CHAPTER 24

I T WAS a bit challenging walking on a spinning street. While it could have been all the drink inside me, I'm pretty sure the way it was so dark didn't help things. The sidewalk looked so cool. There were trees and it was so pretty. Even at night. So cool. I wished I had a camera. I'd take tons of pictures of the trees, and the sidewalk… and the trees…

I managed to get to the concert hall. It looked so cool. I went inside. When the music started, I screamed with the rest of the crowd. The pounding of the drums and the vibrant electric guitar and the bellowing bass was incredible. I wanted to be fucked to the music. I wanted to feel the rhythm pound right through me.

I danced to every song, spinning my body, showing everyone how beautiful I was. I felt like the most beautiful woman in the room. It was so cool.

I felt someone grinding his hips against my butt. I looked over my shoulder and saw a cute guy with glasses. I pressed my butt harder against him. He wrapped his arms around me and squeezed my breasts.

We danced together that way for the whole song. I was so wet for him. It was so cool.

"Let's go to the back," he said in Russian. He took me by the arm. I couldn't wait to have him inside me.

When we reached the back wall, he pressed my body against it and kissed me. His lips tasted peppery. I felt his hands working to unbutton my jeans. He had some difficulty, though, and checked his work.

He scowled. "Are you bleeding?"

I saw that my jeans had a smear of blood on the thigh. It was so cool how worried he was about me. I needed to reassure him. "Don't worry. It's not my blood. It's probably from one of Sukhorukov's guards. I killed him today, but I didn't get hurt. Come on. Let's fuck."

He stumbled and fell backward.

I tried to help him up. "Are you okay?"

"Get away from me!" He scrambled to his feet and slipped away through the crowd.

What was wrong with him? "Loser."

I needed a real man. I stepped back into the crowd to dance.

The band began the song where the two thin women came on stage dancing and stripping off their clothes. I got so excited. I screamed as loud as I could, cheering with everyone else. The singer swayed his hips back and forth as he sang the verses. I moved toward the stage.

At the end of the song, the stage lights flickered.

People chanted, "Kar-lik! Kar-lik! Kar-lik!"

I couldn't wait to see that gorgeous bald muscle man shove his cock inside the midget. I screamed and started chanting with the crowd.

"Kar-lik! Kar-lik! Kar-lik!"

She strutted onstage and we all cheered. The next song started. Then I realized, why should she have all the fun? I rushed to the stage, climbed onto it, and stripped off my T-shirt and jeans. The crowd egged me on so I moved to the music, slowly removing my bra, and peeling off my panties. They cheered louder when I unzipped the singer's pants and pulled out his massive cock. The singer stopped singing. Did he forget the words? I pounced on the singer, wrapping my legs around his torso. He felt like a solid rock of skin.

I screamed. "Fuck me! Fuck me, hard!"

His look of shock changed to a wry smile. I felt him guide his rod to my entrance, then pound into me in time to the opening of the song. I hung on with my arms wrapped around his neck as he hopped along the stage, impaling me on his cock. The crowd cheered and I felt my body flush hot.

I bounced on top of him as he jogged to the center of the stage and hopped in place. I relished this animal taking me, claiming me as his own in front of everyone. Then he stopped and the crowd cheered more. I didn't understand why until little hands pulled open my butt cheeks and I felt a finger wriggle its way into my ass.

It must have been Karlik. Must have been. That was so cool. The singer kept right on pumping me as Karlik's finger tapped the beat alongside the singer's cock.

I screamed out how cool it was. This was the best sex ever. Then the finger was gone but she pried my cheeks open wider and I felt her tongue sliding into my ass. She wasn't just flicking that moist muscle around me, she was literally sticking it inside and lapping at my walls. It was so cool. My body bubbled with fiery goodness and I let my orgasm rumble through my body. The singer hammered faster into me and I felt his cum spray inside me. Warm stream after stream filled me.

Could it get any better than this? I rested my head on his shoulder and he hoisted me up off his cock. I immediately felt the midget's tongue suck out the spunk inside me. She planted her mouth against my channel and I burned with desire as she sucked further and deeper everything inside my pussy. Her tongue swirled into me, lapping up the cream dripping out. When she finished, the singer set me down onto my feet, and the song ended. I could barely stand. I wanted more.

The next song started. I remembered what the thin, naked dancers were about to do. I had to join them. They stood backwards at the edge of the stage. I immediately stood beside one of the thin dancers, both of us with our backs to the crowd. Karlik made a "come hither" gesture with her finger.

Was she going to ask me not to join the naked girls? How could she? This was so cool!

When I bent to put my face closer to hers, she didn't say anything. She just gave me a big kiss, her little tongue darting inside my mouth. I tasted everything. Pussy, cum, sweat, ass, me, her, the singer. The mixture made me giddy.

She let me go. I returned to my pose alongside one of the thin dancers. At the crash of the cymbals, we fell backward onto the crowd of hands. I floated above them all, feeling hands touching me, caressing me, seeking me, exploring me, needing me, demanding me. I wanted more.

Hands held my shoulders, pushed up my back, stroked my arms, squeezed my breasts, grabbed my ankles, rubbed my thighs, groped my butt. Fingers pushed inside my pussy, into my mouth, up my ass, everywhere. As I continued to be passed along from hands to hands, their sensations changed. Some were strong and firm. Some were gentle and supportive. Some were eager and penetrating. Some were loving and soft. I loved them all. I wanted more.

Hands gently lowered me at the back of the room onto my hands and knees, and someone pushed his cock into my mouth. I swallowed it as far as I could, and another entered me from behind. I needed this. I needed it rough and punishing.

I peered up to see the face of the man I was sucking off. With that long, black hair and peachy face, he looked no older than sixteen, though he had to be at least eighteen. They didn't let in anyone under eighteen, did they? He flashed a toothy smile. What a cutie. He held my head and fucked my face. The brutal rawness of his desire for me was so exciting. So healing. And whoever was plugging me from behind was doing an exquisite job. My body swirled in an ocean of tingling joy. He spanked me.

"Yes!" My mouth full of cock tried to speak. "Spank me harder."

He slapped my behind harder, slamming his dick into me. The more my ass stung, the better I felt about myself.

People's hands grazed all over my body, fingers trying to get in my ass, pinching my nipples, guys' hands, girls' hands. I choked on the young man's rod as he continued to shove it deep, in and out of my mouth. He shouted, rammed his cock all the way past my lips, and came down my throat. I swallowed all of his hot, salty fluid relishing the ecstasy I just gave him. I wanted more.

Someone jumped in and I tasted another hard-on between my lips. I licked and sucked, occasionally grabbing his cock in my hands and giving it a good shake down.

Slap!

My ass stung. The guy with his big rod stuffed in my pussy spanked my butt hard. Or maybe it was someone else. It felt so right. My tongue swirled around the tip of the cock in my mouth.

Slap!

Damn, that made my ass prickle. I had behaved so wrong. I deserved this. Using my hand to stroke the man's length at my lips, I managed to get him to spurt into my mouth. I pulled him out and he continued to lash strings of his cum across my cheeks, eyes, and chin. Some blonde girl kissed my lips, licking the cum from my face.

Slap!

Yes! My butt burned. The man behind me cried out and I felt him cream inside me. My blonde girl lifted the dripping cum from my face with her finger and put it to my lips. I gave her finger a brief blow job, each time taking in more of the man's spunk from behind.

Someone picked me up off the floor and wrapped my legs around his torso. He squished himself inside me, my pussy a slush of the other men who came in me. Another man's prick pushed at my back door. Yes! A man sandwich! My ass stretched to accommodate him, and I felt on fire. Both cocks pummeled me and I could not tell which I enjoyed more, the punishing pain or the delicious pleasure.

The one in my pussy shot into me. I thought of the guard I shot earlier. The one in my ass kept right on slicing me. I thought of the cook I sliced in the shoulder.

"Harder! Fuck my ass harder!" I needed to escape these thoughts.

As the guy behind me pounded my burning butt, a leather-clad punk tweaked my nipple and the blonde girl sucked on my other breast.

"Get away from her" A voice yelled in Russian. It was Pasha. He looked angry. *Good. He can punish me, too, for all I care.*

He grabbed me by the arm and yanked me with a strength I didn't know he had. The cock in my rear slipped out, and Pasha dragged me out of the building. I kept stumbling to keep up. Cum dripped out of me down my thighs. The freezing night air bit my naked skin.

He brought me to his truck and covered me with his jacket. I shrugged it off. He covered me again.

"Leave me alone." I shrugged it off again. I wanted the punishment of the cold air. I deserved it.

"Get in the truck," he barked at me. Again, in

Russian. He was no longer practicing his English.

I ignored him and stormed away. He chased after me and grabbed my arm.

"Ow!" My arm hurt from his strong grip.

"What the hell did you do?" He didn't let go of me. "I heard that Sukhorukov was found dead. What did you do?" He seemed to be trying to control his anger.

I yanked my arm free and replied in Russian. "You were wrong, Pasha. What's right and what's wrong is not my choice. I killed a human being. That was wrong."

"Yes that was wrong. So what are you going to do about it? Destroy yourself? Drink yourself to oblivion? Have sex with everyone you meet? Yes, what you did was wrong. But don't let it define who you are. You must live for two people now, Sukhorukov and yourself. Contribute to the community for two people. Enjoy life for two people. What was it you told me? If you can forgive, you can change more than one person's life? You need to forgive yourself. You're a good enough person. You deserve to be forgiven. I know you." He put his hand on my belly. "You killed a man. What do you feel here?"

My gut hollowed. "I feel sick."

He put his hand over my heart. "What do you feel here?"

"Broken." My eyes stung.

"You know why?" His voice quieted, but held the

same intensity. "Because in your heart, you know what's right and what's wrong. Forgive yourself, and you can change a lot of lives. Now get in the truck."

I obeyed his command. As soon as we were both inside, he peeled from the parking space and sped onto the street.

Inside the truck, I smelled alcohol on his breath. "Are you driving drunk?"

He ignored me and muttered, "She kills a man and now she wants to destroy herself." He slammed his fist against the steering wheel breaking off a piece of it. "Why don't you understand? You and I are the same. You don't have to be alone." He swerved to stay in his lane. "Where are you from?" he shouted.

I was suddenly scared. Did he plan on destroying us together? To die together? He had trouble driving straight. He didn't even have his seatbelt on. Neither of us did. He veered off the lane again and then corrected himself.

"Where are you from?" he demanded.

"Kansas! Kansas! Please pull over." I put on my seatbelt.

He sped up, driving across a bridge toward Alexander Park. "Not Kansas. Where are you from?"

"Pasha, you're drunk. At least put on your seatbelt."

He drove faster, weaving in and out of his lane. He scraped a car next to us. It honked.

I felt a lump in my throat. "What are you trying

to do? Get us killed so I can meet your parents?" I right away regretted saying that.

"You and I are the same. You don't believe me? Fine. I'll prove it."

He revved the engine and followed the curve of the road to the other side of the river. He made a sharp left turn into the Peter and Paul Fortress. The truck broke through the wooden gate at the entrance and he drove straight for a tree. In that moment, I realized I wouldn't have enough time to try to get his seatbelt on. I only knew that if I didn't take steps to cushion the coming blow, the crash could be fatal for me, too.

I grabbed the seat cushion beneath me and ripped off a chunk. The truck smashed into the tree. I brought the cushion up to my face to protect myself from the dashboard. Terror strangled me as Pasha's body smashed against the windshield and flew out of the truck. Even with the cushion at my face, the blow against the dashboard felt like I was punched. The seatbelt tugged painfully at my waist. There would be bruising there. That was certain.

When the last of the glass fell and the car stopped moving, I was in a daze. Smoky steam hissed in front of my face. The seat had me squished inside the car.

Pasha!

I groped for the door handle and tried to open it. It didn't budge. I shoved the entire door off with a nudge from my shoulder. The car door crashed to the ground. Ripping off the seat belt, I stepped out of the mangled metal and rushed in front of the car's headlights, fearing I'd find Pasha's dead body.

Pasha stepped out from the darkness and into the light of the headlights.

How was that possible? "You're not injured."

"Neither are you." He took me in his arms and picked me up off my feet.

I realized I wasn't the only one off my feet. The cold air rushed past me. He raised me higher into the air. We were flying!

He said, "I'm from the planet Sarst. Here, they call it Kepler-22 in the Cygnus constellation. Where are you from?"

That was why he kept saying we were the same.

We were both not human.

What did that mean?

Did I finally find someone whose life would never be in jeopardy?

That's why he didn't fear death. He wasn't suicidal. He was invincible.

I could let my love for Pasha blossom into the relationship I longed for my whole life. My dream had come true.

I hadn't answered his question of where I was from. Though I was truly from Kansas, I'd explain to him all about my ancestors another time.

"Just hold me," I said.

He kissed me. All of my sadness dripped away. He

squeezed me against his chest and carried me higher in his arms, above the fortress's colorful spires all lit up, above the Russian rivers and bridges, above the fear that I could never have a man in my life. I held on tighter to his solid chest and shoulders, and in the freezing chill of the night, I felt warmer inside than I ever had before.

# CHAPTER 25

*Cozy Cabins Campsite*
*Near Langley, Virginia*
*Ten months later*

I LOVED waking up to the scent of the fresh pine air. I reached out. The bed sheets were cold. Where was Pasha? Not in our bed. I smelled bacon. Was he cooking?

I stretched and my chest warmed at the thought of this being *our* bed. Wow. Technically, the bed wasn't ours—we had rented the cabin to celebrate our tenth month of being together. But still, to be able to say, "our bed." That felt as good as I had dreamed.

After becoming lovers, Pasha and I hadn't just talk about each other's super powers, we had also revealed to each other our inner most desires and fantasies, ones which we had never revealed to anyone else.

We couldn't keep our hands off each other ever since we'd became an item in St. Petersburg, graduated from college, then came to the United States to take over my Mom's station on the national level of the CIA. Our lovemaking these past months had been relentless, passionate, and unending. Pasha seemed to have energizer bunnies in his lustful eyes and pants. The way he liked to rip my clothes off, I went through more lingerie than a Victoria Secrets catalogue. The more I thought about it, the more I wanted him inside me again.

I flipped over the auburn comforter, and got out of bed not bothering to change out of my long nightshirt and panties.

I stepped to the kitchen and for a second couldn't understand what I was seeing.

Pasha sat bound to a chair in the center of the kitchen, and John, the young man who rented the cabin out to us, held a knife to Pasha's throat. John's back was to me.

"Please," Pasha said in a weak voice. "Do not hurt us."

John turned to me and grinned an off-balance grin. "Don't worry, lady. I won't hurt a hair of your boyfriend here as long as you do what I say."

Pasha had on just his boxers, but his bare chest

was covered with stripes of rope, his arms tied behind his back.

Should I be scared?

I put my hands on my hips. "What's going on?" I asked Pasha.

Pasha shrugged the best he could in his binds. "John used his key to enter as I was making you breakfast."

John placed the blade closer to Pasha's neck, "Shut up!"

But Pasha continued addressing me. "A couple of weeks ago you said you might be into a little role play." He winked.

"What?" John shouted. "Shut the hell up!"

I smelled the bacon, scrambled eggs, and warm toast. My heart warmed. He did make breakfast for me. How thoughtful. I turned off the stove before the bacon and eggs could burn.

"Hey!" John yelled.

I glanced at him.

John pointed at me with his free hand. "Don't move."

"Well, I didn't want the food to burn," I explained.

"It's not the eggs you should be worried about." He pressed the knife against Pasha's cheek, but frowned when he couldn't cut through Pasha's skin.

Pasha spoke with something akin to a stammer, "Please do not hurt me."

I smirked. Pasha was good at many things, but he was a lousy actor.

My cell phone on the kitchen counter rang. I stepped to the counter and bent over the phone to see who was calling.

John said, "Don't answer it, or I'll cut your boyfriend's throat."

It was Langley.

"I have to get this." I answered the phone. "Yeah?"

As John struggled to slice Pasha's throat, muttering and swearing under his breath, Stephen, my handler, spoke on the line. "Sorry to interrupt your vacation, but your mother's overseas on a mission and we've got an arms smuggling operation in Florida we need you and Pasha to deal with."

John must have given up on Pasha because he came at me with his knife. Pasha may have indestructible skin, but not me. I swatted his knife-wielding hand away. John yelped in pain and dropped the knife.

Stephen asked, "Am I interrupting something?"

"Not at all. When do you need us?"

John picked up the frying pan of eggs.

Stephen said, "We're having a debrief at three o'clock. Should we send a chopper your way?"

John ran at me holding the pan like a bat, the eggs spilling to the floor.

"No need." I dodged John's swing, and punched

the side of his head. He fell to the ground unconscious. "Pasha can fly us over there."

"Good. See you then."

"Great." I touched my necklace, the triangular medallion symbol of my ancestors. "The next time you hear from Mom, tell her that Pasha and I send her our love."

"We're not a greeting card company, Ariel. We're the CIA. We do not 'send love.' But I will send her your regards."

I laughed. "That'll have to do."

I hung up and placed the phone on the kitchen counter. "That was kind of fun, Pasha, seeing you play the lady in distress." I removed the cabin keys from John's pocket, flung him out the door like a rag doll, and locked him out.

"I wish only to please you." Pasha gave me his irresistible smile. "That was Stephen on the phone?"

"Yes." I sat in his lap and filled him in on the call. "We have a few hours left to enjoy the rest of our vacation." I traced the ropes bound tight against his chest. "You know, you look pretty yummy all tied up like this."

I kissed him and felt his bulge press against my behind. He returned the kiss, passionate and fierce. That got my blood pumping. Together for ten months and still my heartbeat raced at his kiss.

He slipped his tongue between my lips. I tasted his desire. Could he taste mine?

I broke the kiss and adjusted myself to straddle him on his lap, my legs open to him. I embraced him and we returned to drinking in each other's desire. Lips against lips. My nipples hardening against his chest.

What else was hardening?

I slid a hand down his torso, the ropes rough against my palm, and I reached between my legs, freeing his cock from his boxers. Taking him in my fist, I squeezed. He moaned.

Back when we first played, he said he liked to be squeezed. The harder, the better.

As I sat in his lap, I squeezed his cock harder than any woman could. Watching his eyes drift back in ecstasy, my heart pumped at the power I had over him in my hand. So I pumped him in time with my heartbeat. His breathing quickened.

I slid my other hand inside my panties and stroked myself. Mmm. The tingling that my fingertips spurred on added to the heat I felt from watching Pasha writhe.

I moved to the floor getting on my knees. "You may be indestructible to knives, but just how indestructible are you to kisses?"

He laughed.

I kissed his tip. He sucked in a breath. He looked at me with wide eyes, then sported a bashful grin. He must have known what was coming next.

I kissed his tip again.

He growled. "You are destroying me."

This time I laughed, and then took my poor darling into my mouth. I swirled my tongue around his crown, his musky taste and scent made me giddy. I stuffed two fingers inside me and slid my head down on his length, developing a rhythm. As his thick cock dipped further down my throat, my fingers buried deeper inside me.

He groaned. "If you keep doing that, I will explode."

I let his engorged length bob out from my lips. "Not yet." I grinned.

Of course, I had tasted his delicious cum many times in the last ten months. Different from human men, his tasted tangy, not salty, and after five seconds popped like tiny rock candy in my mouth. A tart and tingling treat. This time, I wanted to feel him inside me.

Shedding my night shirt and whisking off my panties, I crouched above him ready to straddle him again, and guided him to my entrance.

I paused. "If you thought my tongue destroyed you, just wait to see how else I can destroy you, Mr. Indestructible."

I eased down, closing my eyes to the incredible sensation of him filling me with his thickness. I gasped. He growled.

I had to see his face.

Opening my eyes, I inched back up, kept his tip

inside, and squeezed.

He scrunched his face as if in agony. "I cannot take it any more."

He clenched his arm muscles, arched his back, and shouted out a cry of raw animalism, ripping the ropes at his chest. He yanked his arms out of his binds and held me tight. He pressed his bare torso against mine and pushed his full length inside me.

The pleasure pounded through my body.

I could come home each day to Pasha. He could care for me, admire me, adore me, and love me. And be inside me, the way I had him inside me now.

I felt as though I were floating in air. Then I saw how far off the ground we were. Hovering a foot above the ground, Pasha carried me to the bedroom. Still inside me, he lay me down on the bed and rested his weight on top of me.

He pushed in, a slow to and fro, as though caressing me inside.

This was real, I told myself. Pasha stirred the desire inside me, and my body found peace within.

He pushed in and cradled my head. I shuddered by his gaze. It happened every time we made love. By looking deep into those chestnut eyes of his, I felt truly naked. As if he saw more of me than I had ever let anyone see before.

He pushed in, that slow movement becoming a caress comforting me that everything would be okay.

His solid body served as a reminder of how real he

was. How real my future was of coming home into his arms, of feeling his kiss welcome me and love me.

He thrust faster, stronger, pounding himself into me, awakening the dormant fire in my body. My thoughts spiraled out of control. I ached wet for more.

He gave himself to me, hammering inside me his devotion. I arched my back, meeting his thrusts, my desire whirling inside me. Reeling, writhing, embracing.

He cried out and filled me with hot splashes of his seed.

I clenched the sheets, bracing for my coming climax.

Five.

He squeezed my breasts, and the fire at my nipples ignited across my skin.

Four.

I shouted his name. Pasha. The man who would always drive me this wild. My muscles tightened. My toes curled.

Three.

My core clenched around his cock, and my legs and chest shook off the bed, riding out this beautiful orgasm.

Two.

Pasha held me tight. The aftershocks of my orgasm sent tiny tremors across my body, as though foreshadowing the best to come.

One.

Pasha's cum popped inside me, triggering unbelievable shots of pleasure. I screamed during my second climax, letting the power of Pasha's love wash through me. Like tiny firecrackers, the popping continued. Wave after wave took me. I twisted in his arms, loving the buzz that drilled inside me in the form of petite explosions.

I came down after the fireworks, relaxed and loose. We cuddled, no words needed.

I had always thought secrets destroyed relationships, but now I knew that secrets could be the glue to hold a relationship together.

Pasha's warm skin harmonized with the warmth radiating from within me, stemming from the best lesson I had ever learned. Share your deepest secrets with the one you love, and your bond will last a lifetime.

# A PERSONAL MESSAGE FROM THE AUTHOR

Thank you for reading my personal superhero fantasy. I believe that promiscuity doesn't break up marriages, secrets do. I had a thrill working out a situation where secrets actually bring a couple closer together. The truth is every one of us can get more intimate with the ones we love by simply sharing our innermost secrets with him or her. Easier said than done, right? As scary as it is, I hope you find your courage to share your secrets with your beloved. If you do, you'll certainly be a superhero in my book. Speaking of books, what did you think of my story? If you liked it, please write me a review, and share the title with your friends. Whenever I read a great review, my whole day becomes beautiful and I feel like I'm flying. In a way, you can make me feel like a superhero.

Thanks for reading,
Liz Adams

# ABOUT THE AUTHOR

Liz Adams, bestselling author of the erotic fairy tale *Alice's Sexual Discovery in a Wonderful Land*, lives in the San Francisco Bay Area, CA. Her short story *Amy "Red" Riding's Hood*, an erotic version of *Red Riding Hood*, is an Amazon bestseller and winner of Goodreads' Book of the Month for October 2012. Her modern day erotic version of Goldilocks, *Goldie's Locks and the Three Men,* is also a bestseller. Liz studied music and creative writing at UCLA and worked as a freelance model before making her writing her career. In her spare time she cuddles with her spouse on the couch to watch her favorite shows and often they work together doing hands-on research for her books.

If you enjoyed *Ariel's Super Power of Love: The Erotic Wonders of a Super Heroic Woman*, please write a review on Amazon and/or Goodreads! Also, Liz would love to know how you heard about her book, so drop her a line at LizAdamsBooks@gmail.com or at her website www.LizAdamsAuthor.com.

Also by

# LIZ ADAMS

### Fairy Tale Erotica

Alice's Sexual Discovery in a Wonderful Land

(Alice's Erotic Adventures Book 1)

*What will you discover down the rabbit hole?*

Alice's Erotic Adventures through the Mirror

(Alice's Erotic Adventures Book 2)

*If you met your true self, would you recognize her?*

Alice's Story of O:

An Erotic Retelling of The Princess and the Pea

(Alice's Erotic Adventures Book 3)

A Choose-Your-Own-Spice Adventure

*How taboo are you willing to go?*

Goldie's Locks and the Three Men

(A Modern Erotic Fairy Tale Fantasy for Women)

*What if the only way to find the right man*

*was to instead find the right men?*

## Short Stories

Amy "Red" Riding's Hood

(Fairy Tale Erotica)

Hansel & Gretel and the Sexual Hunter

(A Modern Erotic Fairy Tale)

Alina Said, Call Me Maybe

(A Short Romance)


## Short Stories in Anthologies

"Squirting Secrets" in *Campus Sexploits 3:*
*Naughty Tales of Wild Girls in College*

(Out of Print!)

"College Sex with a Foreign Exchange Student, the
Universal Language" in *Campus Sexploits 4*

(Out of Print!)

"The Artist" in *Sensexual: A Unique Anthology*
*2013 Vol 1*

(Urban Fantasy)